Vinayak Mohan is an engineer working in the Middle East (UAE) for the past eleven years. He had the idea of writing a book and his conception finally came to life in 2021. Vinayak is a daydreamer, lost in his dream world. A misfit who never really fits in any crowd always wondering about the possibilities of his life. A quiet philosopher who believes that a better life awaits us all. Vinayak is such a seeker who always is looking to become his better version, always seeking to decipher the mystical world lost in his thoughts, living this human life asking for his life's purpose and meaning.

I would like to dedicate this book to, firstly, my father, the rock star.

To Suchetha Mohan, Devika Mohan and Leela Swaminathan, my mother, sister and grandmother.

To my uncles, MV Ganesh, JS Jayan and Murugan Swaminathan, who supported us over the years, our pillars.

My cousin Suman Haridas and Divya Suman, my sister-in-law, for putting up with me for the past ten years.

To Vinod Vijayan, my best friend.

Finally, to all the misfits, underdogs, dreamers, and the ones struggling to make it in this chaotic life, I'd say it's just a matter of time, keep believing in yourselves.

Vinayak Mohan Cholapurath

## SOUL STORY

AUSTIN MACAULEY PUBLISHERS™
LONDON • CAMBRIDGE • NEW YORK • SHARJAH

**Copyright © Vinayak Mohan Cholapurath 2023**

The right of Vinayak Mohan Cholapurath to be identified as author of this work has been asserted by the author in accordance with Federal Law No. (7) of UAE, Year 2002, Concerning Copyrights and Neighboring Rights.

All rights reserved. No part of this publication may be reproduced, stored in a retrieval system, or transmitted in any form or by any means, electronic, mechanical, photocopying, recording, or otherwise, without the prior permission of the publishers.

Any person who commits any unauthorized act in relation to this publication may be liable to legal prosecution and civil claims for damages.

The age group that matches the content of the books has been classified according to the age classification system issued by the Ministry of Culture and Youth.

This is a work of fiction. Names, characters, businesses, places, events, locales, and incidents are either the products of the author's imagination or used in a fictitious manner. Any resemblance to actual persons, living or dead, or actual events is purely coincidental.

ISBN 9789948798415 (Paperback)
ISBN 9789948798422 (E-Book)

Application Number: MC-10-01-3442247
Age Classification: 17+

Printer Name: iPrint Global Ltd
Printer Address: Witchford, England

First Published 2023
AUSTIN MACAULEY PUBLISHERS FZE
Sharjah Publishing City
P.O Box [519201]
Sharjah, UAE
www.austinmacauley.ae
+971 655 95 202

I would like to express my deepest gratitude to Austin Macaulay for publishing my book. I thank the editors, the production and marketing team and every person who has helped to make this book possible.

To all my readers who have purchased my book, thank you from the bottom of my heart and hope my book has entertained you, motivated, inspired you and transformed you. I hope the best in your journey to discover the secrets hidden in your soul, stay dreaming, keep seeking and don't stop believing.

# Table of Contents

| | |
|---|---:|
| Chapter 1: What If? | 11 |
| Chapter 2: Girl in the Black Skirt | 38 |
| Chapter 3: Father, Oh Father, Where Art Thou? | 62 |
| Chapter 4: I Want to Know What Love Is | 80 |
| Chapter 5: The Shaman | 95 |
| Chapter 6: Way Back Home | 118 |
| Chapter 7: Haunting in Lake View Resort | 137 |
| Chapter 8: Weather Forecast – Depression | 148 |
| Chapter 9: Fallen Prince | 164 |
| Chapter 10: Dark Night of the Soul | 175 |
| Chapter 11: The Calm After the Storm | 191 |
| Chapter 12: Soul Story | 206 |

# Chapter 1
# What If?

I am on my way to buy a fishbowl and two goldfish. To be honest, I wanted a puppy, an English bulldog to be precise, but apparently, pet dogs are expensive where I live and English bulldogs are very, very expensive. I live in, hmmm, let's call the place Wonderland, I have been living in Wonderland for the past ten years. *God, how time flies, where did all the time go*, I wonder. Time is a strange concept, we cannot get back the time lost and cannot access the infinite time available in the future, and to make matters even more complicated, we humans are mortal so we have a finite amount of time we live, but, we cannot know how much time we have 'cause death can happen at any instant, time flows, and you have created a past which can only be remembered, and you cannot tamper with the time gone. The only instance you have control is at the present moment, and what you decide to do in that moment means everything as it decides the path you lay for the time to come. The only evidence of the time that has passed for me is my increasing waistline, a moment has passed just when you read that and my waistline has managed to increase by a millimeter, that's how aggressive my weight gain has been off late. I wish we lived on a planet where time could be manipulated.

What if, each one of us could go back in time to change something in our past, wouldn't that be great? But then I think why we should be in a planet that allows time manipulation, what if we were an intelligent life form that could control time, an ability we processed as humans? What if we all had the ability to go back to our past, change an event that would change the trajectory of our life in the present and our future. Wait, what was I planning to do now, ah yes, the goldfish. I know I told you I was on my way to the pet store to buy the goldfish and the fishbowl, but I wasn't really being honest. My mind was on its way, but my body is still stuck in bed. My body is saying, let's rest a little longer and then we'll go to the pet store, but my mind is already at the pet store deciding what kind of tank and fish to buy.

Wait a minute, did I just refer to myself as "we" as if my body and my mind were two separate individuals. Trust me, sometimes it does feel like it. Have you ever been in a situation where you gained weight and getting yourself to the gym seemed impossible? Wherein your mind says, you got to go to the gym, and then, your body says, "After this cupcake." And this situation of dissonance between your body and mind goes on for days 'cause your body keeps finding an excuse every day. Then, several cupcakes later one fine day you're looking at the mirror petrified at how you got this fat. Immediately your body says, "You got to go to the gym," and then your mind says, "Dude, what the hell have I been telling you all these days." Finally, you're at the gym working out like an animal and after 14 minutes and 25 seconds into your workout a voice from your heart says, "Wow, I feel like I did enough for today, great job buddy," and then your body's like, "Really, we're done," and the mind's like, "No, no, no keep going." And then the voice from the heart says, "Let's call it a day today and it's a Tuesday, let's start seriously and fully committed on Monday. It just doesn't feel right starting in the middle of the week and we got plans to go out on Saturday night, drinking with the guys, definite weight gain expected so start fresh next week." And even before you know it, you are sitting on the couch eating cupcakes and ordering a pizza to watch, how to lose weight and look like the God of Thunder.

I lay in bed trying to quiet my mind so I can get a few more minutes or maybe an hour of sleep and then definitely go to the pet shop. Wait, what's the time? WHAT! It's just 6:30 in the morning, two hrs. of sleep then. Ya, but no pet store opens at 8:30 in the morning, they all open at 10:00. Great then three hrs. of sleep. What about going to the gym, screw the gym today, today is Sunday, it's rest day. SSHHHHHSSOOOSH GO TO SLEEP. After a few seconds, Tu Ta TU utu hm tu ta tu TUU TU, I wonder what I'll name my fish. Goldie and Holdie, Goldie and Holdie, really? How about Goo and Boo. Wait a minute, maybe my future self will come and tell me the names. I guess apart from time control, we should also have the power to teleport. What if Gandhi decided moments before his death to go back into his past and change the course of his life. I wonder what would have happened to India's independence. The world would have never been introduced to the concept of winning independence by non-violence, or what if he used his power to dodge the bullets that killed him. But wouldn't have the killer too seen that in his future, this is so complicated.

Thinking about it, what if Hitler used his time control power to win the war. Wonder what the world would be like then. I guess then every soldier would have known about their own death, thus giving them the insight to save themselves at that moment, and the war would have gone on, and on, and on, 'cause each side has the power to change the future. Maybe the Americans would have come up with a device or an antidote that would completely stop humans from their ability to time travel and stopped Hitler anyway. What if Hitler found that out and then made himself an anti-anti-dote that would make him immune to the anti-dote and then become the only person who can time travel. This is complicated, right? Maybe I'll restrict these powers to just me. I'd say time control and teleportation would be great. The only human in the universe who can control time and teleport. I wonder if there's life on the other universes and if there was life, what would they look like. Or what if the multiverse was a mirror of our universe existing at different points in time. Maybe the world war has just started in one and the dinosaurs are still walking on another. Maybe there are universes I am an old man in and others where I have died, and maybe I am just about to be incarnated on another universe.

What if they were all different and unique and had nothing common to each other then we would be the only ones in the multiverse, the only universe with life since none of the other universes would have any characteristic in common, then would there be more life forms on other planets in our own galaxy apart from Earth, and if there was, I'm very open to meeting them, because I am curious what they would be like. Imagine finally getting to meet an alien woman with four tits and they all are Claudia Schiffer like, I'm just kidding but yes,

I wonder what they would be like. So how many galaxies are there in our universe. Google how many galaxies are there in our universe. Google says there are about 125 billion galaxies. Phew, that's a lot, I wonder if I started counting from the moment of my birth, would I be able to count to 125 billion before my death? Hmm, okay, let us assume I had the divine gift of counting at the time of birth, and I had the ability to cover a number in a second then I would take 125 billion seconds to accomplish the task, if I never had a break and just kept counting until death. I wonder how many minutes that would be. Where is my phone, hmm, calculator, how many zeros in a billion, google says 9 so 125,000,000,000 divided by 60 would give me 2,083,333,333.33 mins, divide that by another 60 would give me 34,722,222.22 hours, divide that by 24 that would be 1,446,759.25 days, divide that by 30 would give me 48,225.3 months and divide that by 12 would give me 4018.8 years, roughly, assuming all months have 30 days and there were no leap years.

So, I would have to live for 4018.8 years to finish counting to 125 billion. Can't keep my mind concentrated on one task for a few minutes wonder how I will concentrate for 4018.8 years to just count. Now why did all these calculations start, ah, yes, the number of galaxies in our universe, I guess the sheer number of galaxies alone gives us a high probability of finding life in our universe. That is not taking into consideration of all the UFO's claimed to have been seen by various people over the history of our planet Earth. This alone increases the probability of life existing in at least one other planet out there among the 125 billion galaxies in our universe, I wonder why the governments are hiding this from us, if aliens did visit Earth, I believe it is our right to know, all of us should know, I would love to know more about them and I've got a ton of questions to ask them, the governments shouldn't be hiding anything from us. How could anybody make up something such as an Alien until you saw one for real. Is it possible for man to come up with an original idea or concept that never existed in the universe or all the other universes, is it possible for the human mind to create something up that never existed at all, for example lets imagine fish never existed? Can the human mind now imagine something like a fish, make it up just by pure imagination?

Maybe he can arrive at imagining a fish by observing birds and wondering if there was a similar or different form of life that lived in water. And by asking himself, what would that look like, he could arrive at an idea of a life form that could live in water, but then to sketch it he will once again have to draw something that looks like a bird but in water. Now, I am asking can us humans come up with the idea of aliens unless, an alien was seen for real? Or if, the idea came to existence by wondering if life was happening here on earth could there be life forms on other planets. And if there was life on other planets, what would they look like? Are authentic or original ideas conceived from observing nature and then exaggerated by the human imagination. Or are humans genuinely capable to conceive authentic ideas and concepts that never existed anywhere in the universe. Can you imagine an alien purely out of imagination or was the idea sparked by comparison? Even then the aliens came by spaceships or UFO's or flying saucers, whatever, then how could man document a spaceship in the form of engravings in caves and drawings on stone walls at a time when humans rode animals as a mean of transportation. How did the early man imagine

UFO's when there wasn't any technological advancement to that scale at that time? But then Hinduism has epic stories like Ramayana that speaks of flying objects dated back sometime between the 6$^{th}$ and 7$^{th}$ BCE.

Evidence of aliens on our plant dates back centuries. Google 'earliest evidence of aliens on Earth' search. Google has tons of articles on alien presence on our Earth dating back centuries. But to what extend are these articles true. Ah, don't you just wish you had the power to go back in time to find the truth. What is the time now? What! 9:45, I hate this, every time I try to sleep I just can't. Wish I had an off button for my mind. Now I don't even want to get out of bed, but I have too. Need to buy them gold fishes, Goldie and Holdie, seriously? Goldie and Holdie? I need to find new names. Maybe I'll get a golden one and a black one and then call them Orange and Black. Oh yes, I'm calling them Thunder and Lighting, and I'll get a black one and a white one.

"*Thunder, feel the thunder, lighting and the thunder.*" Oh boy that was a good song. So, its official my gold fish will be called Lighting and Thunder. Finally, after much effort I got my head of the pillow and sat upright on my bed staring at the bathroom door wondering how I'll get all the way there. The urge to smoke a cigarette got me out of bed. I grabbed my cigarettes and headed to the balcony thinking what Juliana would be doing. Juliana is my neighbor from Ukraine, moreover, a goddess from Ukraine. Words cannot describe Juliana. The first time I laid my eyes on her I wasn't sure if I was hungry, or she made me horny. Maybe I was so horny it made me hungry. She does yoga on her balcony and it's like watching a thousand sunsets, all at one time. The way she looks in her yoga pants sends all sorts of electrical signals down my body, trust me, she is a total bomb and watching her do yoga makes me feel all better, my stress disappears, and it gets me ready for work. The air around her, itself, is different, it smelt like spring just arrived and once she walks by everything blossomed. Her hypnotizing brown eyes will stop you in your path like a deer stun by the light. It always feels like time slows down, and she moves in slow motion, slowing everything she passes by. The first time I encountered her was in a lift and it took like forever to get to my floor, because you guessed it, it was in slow motion. Gosh, I'm hungry, let me get a sandwich.

And God, that ass, I was struggling not to speak about it. Oh my God that ass, perfection, perfection I'd say. Her hair, how her golden blond hair flows down on her back. Starts yellow and golden and then just flows into her back and ends halfway. The curves on her as sexy as a formula on track, I dream that I'm Michael Schumacher in my Ferrari, formula one beast, driving reckless and fast down those curves, all day, and all night long. Phew, I have seen many men stand with boners while she walked past them in the supermarket. Once the cashier at the cash register said, "Dude you're missing the show," and when I turned around there she was walking down from the vegetable and fruit aisle in slow motion, it was like everything around her stopped and everyone was looking at her, old people, married women, married men, bachelors, kids, and even a baby on the tit feeding pushed her mother's boob away and was like gggooo gaaagaa (since everything was in slow motion so was the sound) and right then I noticed all the men in that area standing with boners so strong poking out their trousers. And a couple of boys all almost hitting puberty popped like pop corns becoming young men looking perplexed down their shorts thinking to themselves, "IT GROWS."

I remember turning to the cashier and saying I know her, she's, my neighbor. And he gives me a smug smile and, telepathically, he says to me, "You, lucky bastard," and in my mind I replied to him, "Oh, yes, I am that lucky bastard." So, by now you should be getting the idea Juliana is super, super hot. Sitting on the balcony I realized the time was 10:00 am now, where is my tea. Let me give you an idea of how it is going to go down, I'm going to make my tea and then get ready to go out to the pet shop. Staring at my kettle waiting for the water to boil I begin to think about my life. I dream of being successful in a ridiculously massive scale, but I still have no clue what I should be doing. Why do I struggle to know what my passion is? Why do I seem so lost? I always dreamt when I was little, I would be doing great things that would change the world. Why is life so impossible to catch a break? What am I doing wrong? What must I be doing? So many questions flew past my head and the years are flying by too, making me feel like a bum but a year older each year. Maybe I wasn't cut out for fame or success. I wish I could turn every part of me around and achieve the impossible but that thought seems to stay just in my dreams.

I returned to the balcony sipping my tea wondering if I will ever achieve my dreams or will I drift through life being a nobody. *Enough of thinking*, I thought to myself, I got to get ready. On the way to the pet store, I could not stop wondering what meaning there is to life. What is the purpose of life? Why is there life at all? And why are there so many forms of life? What does all this mean? Is there a reason a purpose for life to happen? Now that I'm here, what is my purpose? Why am

I here? And why does, whatever I'm doing currently in my life, feel like it's not what I'm meant to be doing. Are we all created to contribute to something greater than ourselves, like for God, or are we meant to just live by our wants and needs and make life up as we go on about it? Are we meant to follow what society says? Are we meant to believe in a God and follow his teachings? Is there a God? Why is he so shy to reveal himself? Why is that he came centuries, and centuries ago and why isn't he visiting us now? Is he that far away? Is he tired or maybe wounded? Did he forsake us? Or has he created life somewhere else and perfected his creation learning from our short comings. Or is he just interested in creating life and moving on to the next venture? Creating one universe after the other. Or maybe there isn't one and everything evolved like our scientists say. The big bang, plants forming and then evolution happening on our planet like the Darwin's theory. What do we know for sure? Who do we ask? Why didn't God leave someone behind to teach us all. You'd say Jesus, Krishna and so forth yes but why aren't they here now? Why did they have to die? And when they did die, why didn't they come back?

Why didn't God leave someone like Jesus or Krishna to rule the world, so we are guided and steered in the right direction but instead left us behind with people who just wanted to conquer out of ambition, greed, power and what all misery has the Earth faced. And why most of us don't stand up against the few who dictate and tell us how to live and where to live. Democracy is a joke in my perspective. Because our leaders are influenced by the wealthy ones. And whenever an honest man who truly want to serve the people comes along is assassinated. Today's world is all about money, its owned by businesses. Who said we needed jobs and currencies and passports and taxes? The education system now a days is a farm where slaves are manufactured and used as batteries for multinational companies and business organizations to make more money for them. We are paid for what they think we are worth; we are taxed based on what they think we ought to pay. Despite all our technologically advances life has only got more and more complicated. Medicines are expensive, building a new house is very expensive, education is expensive I can go on and on and on. It's almost like we are paying to cover up someone else's losses that we are unaware of. Who sits and decides the price for material stuff? How do we know that it's what it should really cost? Maybe the true cost of manufacturing a smart phone is just 100 dollars and they are selling it for 1000 dollars. I don't know. Do you? Do we really know the true price for what we are paying for? Take that question metaphorically as well.

What does poor Juliana know, I bet she's clueless on these matters, all she cares about is making more and more money to maintain a lifestyle she can't afford and to get the attention of men who can help her sustain the lifestyle she seeks but who'll probable break her heart and then eventually she'll join a feminist group or a trip to India to rediscover her true self. Maybe Yuliana's true self wants something else altogether, but she doesn't know it yet because she's been programmed the minute she was born. Maybe I'm wrong. Maybe this is how it's meant to be. Maybe God created us flawed in certain ways. Maybe it's his dark sense of humor because we have got too serious with life that we don't stop to think about anything. Most of us are running on fear, fear of paying the bills, getting a degree, chasing a dream, we are so self-absorbed in our own fabricated fear filled life that we have lost the ability to shut down and look beyond our small petty minds and feel alive. Do you feel the life in you? Do you truly feel alive? Ask yourself? What would become of this system if we all quit to find our true purpose. What would happen to these Multinational corporations, oil companies etc. etc. What if we all found our unique way to live. What would these business owners do?

Don't listen to anything I have to say. I'm just a crazy guy who thinks too much. Don't let my ramblings affect you. Maybe all these rules and restrictions are put in place to create some order. Maybe without them the world would be in true chaos. I guess we humans aren't evolved enough to take care of ourselves without someone policing us. These rules put in place might be the only reason stopping us from tearing each other apart. We haven't consciously evolved enough to see all humans and all living things as equals and share this planet and live-in harmony. Despite how advanced we think we have become we haven't evolved enough to be humane to each other. Wars are still being fought, discrimination against color still happens, women still fight for equality. There might be no other way for humans to co-exist until there are laws and there is a body assigned to enforce them. Maybe we ought to fix that first before our countries use secretly built weapons that can wipe us out in minutes.

At the pet shop my mind suddenly shut down. Felt like I was at the zoo for domestic animals. I was focused cause I knew if I spent a lot of time, I would have left with a puppy which I clearly can't afford. So, I went straight to the fish section got a white bubble head or what you call an Oranda. It had a nice orange head with a white body and then a black

Moor fish. Got a regular sized bowl with, two-gallon capacity. While walking back to the car I felt excitement grow in me, I felt like I'd just accomplished something big, I am going to be daddy to two fish. These two fish would be my first pets. Never have I dreamt of the day that I would buy my pet fish. Can't even understand why I would go through with it. I wanted an English bull puppy and here I am with two goldfish. Suddenly, I began feeling more responsible, I would have two other living beings to take care of. The feeling that I'd have company when I reach back home in the form of fish made my heart feel warm. I looked at the two fish closely wondering how our lives were destined to meet. Our lives have entangled to each other now, I felt a strange sense of joy as I looked at these fascinating creatures. My fish Thunder and Lighting. *Thunder, feel the thunder, lightning and the thunder* (singing to myself).

*Wow*, I never thought having a pet would bring so much joy. My heart was filling itself up with love for my goldfish. *Gosh*, I thought, *I own, and I am responsible for two other living fish, I'm so EXCITED*. Got in the car and drove away from the pet store blasting the music and feeling on top of the world. Felt like I've accomplished something so big it made me feel AWESOME. Wait a minute did I buy the fish feed. Made a U-turn, drove back to the pet store, rushed to the counter, bought the feed, ran back to the car, and drove away blasting the music feeling AWESOME all over again, Woo-hoo, totally nailed today. Need to start saving for my puppy next.

Back in the den, I set up the fish tank, sitting on my couch I was looking at my new company in admiration. Felt like I've climbed Everest and felt very accomplished for the day it was time to move on to the next task. But I haven't had enough looking at my fish, so I kept glancing at them now and then. A smile would crack on my face as I stared at them with absolute adoration. *My babies*, I thought to myself. I wonder what they would be telling me if they could talk. Strange isn't it how we humans have the tendency to cage animals just for their fascination. Somehow, we need to cage them to study them or love them to fulfil our curiosity or need for company. I wonder who bestowed this privilege to enable us to do so.

How did this concept of having pets start? Was it out of fascination and curiosity? or was it out of love to protect them? Why do we have this urge to cage? Why don't we love them from their own habitat? Why do we need to bring them into our space? Train them in some cases, groom them, feed them. Despite the hardships people still have, they still have the capacity to take up additional responsibility in the form of pets.

I wonder if planet Earth is the fishbowl for human beings. What if a super being or an alien race is looking at us from afar in admiration just as I was looking at my goldfish? What if we were put here by the alien race as their pets. What if we were bought from a universal pet shop and brought here to planet earth? And just like rabbits we just multiplied so fast. And what if the Alien guy up there came back after a millennium, shocked to see so many of us? And how we evolved so much, the internet, travel to the moon and Mars, aeroplanes, bullet trains, the Burj Khalifa and the atomic bomb. I would really love to see the alien's face, he would be so shocked, and surprised, and his big alien brain blown out of the milky way. Let's call our Alien Bob. Bob would be like woah they can fly, what they have left the planet, oh no they keep pets too. Well, the thing about Bob is time works differently for him a year in Bob's life would be like 1000 centuries for humans. So, Bob would have got to see us evolve is such a fast pace his brain would be truly blown out of his mind. He just wouldn't be able to imagine how something so tiny was capable of such wondrous and miraculous things.

What if you came home one day to find that your gold fish have multiplied to a few hundred, but they all fit in that water bowl, magically, they have built roads and hospitals and is planning to build a water shuttle that will take them to the mysterious space they keep seeing outside their fishbowl. Schools for the little ones, discos for the young. Wouldn't that blow your mind. Gosh I would be so blown away I wouldn't know how to react. My favorite part would have been to meet their celebrities, Brad Fish wonder what he would look like.

Are we gold fish to God or a mysterious alien race that doesn't need to show up often because we figured out a way to survive beautifully? Sounds stupid but I'm just saying what if this was the situation. I wish I knew all the secrets of the universe then writing this book would be far easier. I bet the book would have practically written itself. Why is that you struggle the most when you yearn for the things you desire. But when you don't care all your desires turn up with such ease. I wonder what I am not doing to attract the life that I wish. I must get to the bottom of this and figure it out.

Is it true that you attract what you think or to be more precise you attract the way you feel depending on how long you can stay in that state of mind? Is this true? There is a great deal of information available regarding this topic and I wonder if there is any truth to it. I wonder how your emotional state affects you from having wealth, health, or the life you dream off. I have tried everything to make myself feel good and terribly fail to maintain it. Are these universal laws we hear for real, are all the mystics in India actually, right? But when you ask any successful person who you know all they can say is work hard, hard, hard. How do we break illusions of poverty from the mind or the lack of self-worth? They must be illusions right, if abundance too is a possibility at the same moment in time. Meaning there is you living in lack and there is you living in abundance at the same moment in time and the only thing you need to do is choose consciously how you want to live. Is this the truth, cause if there is no time constraint for the universe to manifest anything for you, then where is all the things I asked for? Well, I'm sorry if I've been hammering you with so many questions, trust me I have my reasons in order to understand why, you must know my story.

My story starts in 2011, the year that turned things upside down and twisted way too around in my life. Thought that I hit rock bottom, but the coming years would prove me wrong and take me to newer more creative levels of rock bottoms. This is the year I started my journey to understand the mysteries of the mystical nature of the universe, the magical nature of the universe that can grant our wishes. The dimension where anything is possible, that mysterious space that grants our wishes. Emotionally I cannot explain where I was and how I felt back at that time. I was living in a tornado of pain, fear, guilt, pain, and pain like I cannot describe it to you. The need to medicate was very necessary so I could numb the emotions that went threw me, which was making me sick. I would medicate on various substances and plunge myself into women having meaningless relationships. Don't worry this isn't a depressing story but its where we are going to start. The darkness in me was so evident I literally walked around with a dark cloud above my head which had its own thunderstorm. Some days were so bad it felt like the only agenda the universe had for that day was to screw my life. Now, I felt like this for days, months and eventually years. I just didn't know what was going on. It felt like God robbed me of all my luck and replaced it with a truck load of shit and a tight slap to remind me of the shit luck he has blessed me with.

But somewhere deep, deep, deep inside me from the depths of my soul I had a feeling that I was meant for something big. But the problem was, I was trapped in a depression that just wouldn't go away. And the drinking made sure I stayed trapped in it. My emotional state felt like I was on a barren land rotting and there was a sea of blood between me and to the other side, the side or emotional state I wished to be. The other side which I could see from inside me, projected like a magical tropical land, a very luscious land rich in resources, breath-takingly beautiful with tropical forests, mountains with crystal clear lakes. Man, animals all sharing the land with joy celebrating life. Life was thriving to the fullest, somewhere the sea of blood disappeared to turquoise blue water and waters flowed with such elegance to the shores of this mystical place called life. A place so mystical, pure magic I would say, the people are so welcoming and cheering you to be your best. Beautiful woman walking around with pints offering you a massage while you drank your pint, that magically refilled itself. A place where you're so joyous, free, and drunk with love. Every day is a new adventure exciting, thrilling with a surprisingly wonderful ending. In this place you are the superstar and women want to be with you and your having trouble to choose. And then you wake up and eat whatever you want, and you still have washboard abs. a wonderland, there it was right there on the other side.

The place where I was, I'd say was worse than hell. It was pitch dark, and my heart was in constant pain. A pain so deeply rooted in me that it cracked the protective barrier in me, where the soul rested and now the darkness crept in and was feeding out of the light, growing stronger and scarier by the day. It had its claws so deep in me I no longer knew who I was and what I wanted. My mind was invaded by negative thoughts that just kept adding fuel to a fire that strengthen the depression. Emotions all over the place like waves of blood rising as high as skyscrapers washing everything I tried to build positively. The land was rotten, and everything was dying. The soil all black like tar and blinding darkness. A darkness which I cannot describe by color because this was blacker than black and the blood all redder than red. The air smelled like death and the demons that haunted me took all kinds of shapes and forms keeping me trapped in a loop of torture that kept repeating day in and day out.

And somewhere in this reality I still existed trying to break free, but I did not know where I was, I did not know who I was. Now, all of this existed in me while on planet Earth I took up a job I then hated but stuck by it, because I was still looking for the right kind of opportunity my heart desired. I hated the job not because it was horrible, I hated the job because I was feeling bad about myself. It was meant to be something I'd do temporarily until I figured out what I really wanted to do with my life. But that was a trap I stayed for quiet sometime. I'm never going to talk about the things that went wrong, this book isn't about that. This book it about the journey from there to where I was headed. While being in this meditative depressed state which I thoroughly maintained those years. I got to know the dark side of me. Trust me, it felt like I was possessed and thought of getting an exorcism because I felt my mind and body was taken over by a demon. Only the drinking gave me some relief at least for those drunken hours. Where, the demon gained control and let me feel anything but the usual pain. But little did I know I was only strengthening a whole other beast which would take me on wild crazy nights and then the lowest of morning lows.

I just didn't know where the real me went and wondered who this guy was, seeing through my eyes and thinking through my brain and eating out of my mouth. I have demanded him to take me to the real me and set me free. But my words fell wasted to deaf ears. In the real world I was working my ass off, exercising, trying to get all things right and aligned so I could head in the right direction. But no, the more I tried the harder I fell. I was in a constant state of anxiety and panic and the world was spinning to fast and making me dizzy. This fear inside me which I could not understand what it was had me running and hiding from a shadow that kept following me. My mind constantly in a state of confusion trying to decipher the outwardly influence of the reality I was living in so I could just survive. How did it get to this? I pondered every day, analyzing and reanalyzing, replaying every bit and piece of the past. Angry at myself for having done this to me. I felt all alone, scared cause this was all my fault. I was the one to blame, as I allowed my life to get to this. I criticized and tortured myself, bullying and pushing myself to turn this situation around immediately. I was in such a hurry to save myself, but I only ended up being more entangled in the mess I was creating, thinking that it was all part of the plan to fix my life I managed to fix nothing only messed it up more.

The idea of buying goldfish were non-existed on my head at that time as I could barely take care of myself. Somehow the beacon that was meant to send out the amazing signals to the universe was hacked by this demon and it was sending exactly the opposite signals I hoped for. And this killed me as I felt I had no control over my own self. This feeling of being overpowered by someone else and feeling helpless that I could not do anything about it, persisted in me and was forcibly reshaping my personality and habits. I was fighting this on a second by second, minute by minute basis, trying to stay sane, trying to keep the tower from collapsing because I felt that if I didn't stop it and try to get my life back. I would be gone and washed into the darkness forever. This thought was frightening and made me so anxious that I worked like ten men. The anxiety kept me away from defeat, it kept pushing me to do more and more even if it was a job I dreaded and hated. At least I'm earning money and able to survive I thought. I didn't save a nickel, I spent it all on activities this demon wanted, drinking, parties, bar hopping until early hours in the morning and ending up in hotel rooms with women I couldn't remember meeting the previous night. It really felt like a good time, but the feeling good part could only happen if I was under the influence of some drug or drink, when I became sober in the morning, I would feel very low, depressed, anxious, fear of becoming this person who is spinning out of control.

This was not what I wanted, as I wasn't creating anything beautiful with my life. I wasn't doing the things I was meant to be really doing and the problem was I never even really knew what it is I should be doing. All the luck I had at that time was for situations that only aggravated my current situation which was self-destruction. Let me tell you the story of meeting Venessa, a beautiful Filipino lady. Venessa was working as a nurse at a well-known hospital. Let's call it the "I-hope-you-get-sick-so-we-can-make-money hospital." I'll tell you why later. So, one-night as Venessa was getting dressed for work, she was explaining to her friends Mary, Abbey, and Venus of how tired she was working night shifts and she's so happy that her shift timing will be changing next week, and she wanted to go out the coming weekend to celebrate her change in her shift timing. so, the girls planned to a night out the coming Saturday to meet in Copa Cabana a happening club in Downtown, Wonderland. Meanwhile several miles away from her, to be exact 32 miles, on the following morning, since the night Venessa made plans with her friends. I woke up late having overslept as I was out drinking the whole night with Tania a wonderful Russian lady who I just happened to meet that night. More on Tanya later, so I called office and called the day off, I slept till around after noon and then decided to go out. As I was driving, the urge to have a drink or two, crossed my mind and maybe after that I'll go back to my room and call it a day. So, I turn up to the pub I regularly visit and six pints later the bartender a friend of mine gives me a pass, a ticket to Copa Cabana. He said it was the club to visit and I must go. I reluctantly accepted the ticket though I had no plans to go I kept it for no reason. How do you refuse a free pass to a club right?

And then the weekend comes, completely forgotten about the free pass. I left the office and went for my run got back to my room and sat on my bed wondering what to do for the weekend. The time was 10:00 pm and then I got a call, it was a friend and he asked me to come immediately to Copa cabana, said the place was amazing and I had to come there no matter what. That's when I remembered of the free pass and immediately showered, dressed, and raced to Copa Cabana, not aware what was going to unfold for that night and for the coming weeks. On the way I was caught in traffic, Traffic, I mean traffic like I never seen. Seemed like everyone on the planet was on that route. And I hit the red light on each signal and there was like 20 of them. On any other day I would reach the destination by 25 minutes but that day it took close to an hour. On any other day I would cruise through each signal, and they would magically light up green and I would just drive by, but not on that day. The signal would go green and as I got close to the junction Orange and then Red. And with all the cars that appeared mysteriously on the road that day I was inching the car when nearing the traffic signal, which was very frustrating. I was lighting one cigarette after the other and finally hit the freeway to the city. I did not notice I was over speeding, I just had to get there as soon as possible. A bright light flashed, which was a speeding camera, I thanked the heavens for blessing me with such amazing luck and drove on. Finally, reached the place and found there was no parking anywhere close, so I had to park two blocks down the club and walk back.

Halfway to the club I notice that I have forgotten to take my cigarettes, so I ran back to the car. Did I mention it was summer and the weather was like 42 degrees and the humidity was annoyingly high? Finally reached the car got my cigarettes and walked back two blocks and finally reached the club to discover I forgot to take the pass this time, I prayed that I'll find it in the car. The time was getting close to mid night, so I took a cab to the car got the pass which was luckily there and asked the cab driver to drop me back. Finally, inside the club I was relieved but was soaked in my own sweat smelling delightfully repulsive. I went to the men's rooms freshened up and met my friends. We were four guys sitting on a table close to the dance floor. And as I was settling into my chair feeling like I reached heaven and about to sip my beer. A flash of light fell on my face, and I looked ahead to trace the source, and there she stood. The light reflected of, I don't know what it was a buckle, or a belt made of highly polished metal or glass pieces on her belt, I'm just guessing here, well you get the idea it reflected off a buckle that was part of a very fancy belt that lay around a slender waste, and as my eyes started moving up to see her face she turned around and now all I could see was her back and her friends. She was standing up, don't know what she was doing because she was kind of swaying to the music and making a lot of gestures with her hand. Looked like she was explaining something to her friends. Cause they were all leaning in looking at her and paying attention.

I was sitting exactly across her on the other side of the dance floor waiting for her to turn. Not that I didn't like what I was looking at. She had a gorgeous derriere, and the way that black skirt was hugging to her body was like it was painted on her bare body. And then her belt I don't know what it was, seemed like it was made of glass because it was reflecting light of her hip. I couldn't help but wonder maybe she wore it on purpose so the light that reflected off her belt draws her mate she's looking for. Maybe she was totally unaware of it. I held my gaze wondering when she will turn and I was in no hurry to see her face, as I was enjoying the view of her back swaying to the music. One million thoughts raced through my head in the speed of light that were very explicit in nature the images weren't very clear cause it moved in the speed of light but the emotion that was radiating from my pants knew exactly what those images were.

My friend interrupted my state of trance and in that second when I turned to look at my friend who was shouting in my ears and as my face turned to him trying to understand what he was saying between all the loud music blasting, and the vibrations coming out the speakers behind us, right in that moment, the universe decided to orchestrate the revealing of the mystery woman's face. The universe decided to send Mr. X, I didn't know this gentleman's name so let's call him Mr. X, a man in his mid-forties working for a reputed oil company stumbles into the club. Mr. X had a great day at work and was promoted to be a member of the board of directors. Mr. X was a stout man with balding hair. He resembled a man who was once handsome, but the heavy drinking and unhealthy eating habits took a toll on his handsomeness. Now he looked like a memory of a handsome guy but had this aura of power within him. He was an important guy and had many influential contacts with the cities powerful people. Despite Mr. X's success in this professional life his married life was a disaster. Mrs. X was growing in suspension of Mr. X's whereabouts at night, she even hated that he drank like a fish.

Lately he was returning home late than his usually time. She suspected he was having an affair; she had been patient with his drinking but now infidelity she will not put up for this. So, when Mr. X left for the day's work, she went through his stuff at his home office, she checked every inch of that room and found nothing. Then she went through his wardrobe, found nothing there either. Partially happy she sat on the couch not entirely convinced, sipping her coffee she felt a bubble of suspicion grow stronger inside her. She was sure there was something going on but then her mind argued that there was no proof and it was all her imagination. The poor man works so hard and provides for the family in abundance, she shouldn't be accusing her husband of something that might not be true. But she wasn't convinced completely yet she had to ask him and clear things from her heart and mind as it was eating her up from the inside. She missed the days her husband used to take her out, where did all the love and romance go, she wondered. She walked back to the bedroom and noticed Mr. X's iPad lying on the side table on his side of the bed. She entered his password and found a picture of her and the kids as the background picture for a moment her eyes filled with tears of joy and love for her husband and right that instant a mail came in with the subject "Hey Baby." Her heart started pounding so loud she could hear it; she immediately knew what that mail was all about. I knew it, I knew it, I knew it she kept repeating to herself. And when she opened the mail there it was, pictures and love messages. A Volcano erupted in Mrs. X she no longer was the calm, loving caring woman. She was on fire, and she was out to get his blood.

Meanwhile Mr. X having had a great day at work decides to go home and take his family out to celebrate. He calls Mrs. X but gets no answer, he calls her again she cuts the phone.

This is strange he thought and calls her again this time the phone rings and goes unanswered again. He panics and feels something has happened to his beloved wife. He tries reaching his eldest son on his phone, but he won't pick up either now his suspicion has been confirmed. Something has gone wrong with his family and so he rushes home. When he reaches his apartment on the 21$^{st}$ floor of a luxury apartment that faced the sea, he rang the bell and he waited but there for a while, with no answer, worried and panicked he rings the bell again and then his youngest son opens the door. Mr. X shouts what's wrong, what's wrong, the young lad says nothing and walks into his room. He enters his apartment and walks into the living room. And sees his wife, her face red, from crying, her black eye line dripping down her cheeks, from a distance she looked like she was transforming into a beasty witch. She had that look in her eyes like she wanted to cut his cut manhood off and feed it to his bitch he was having an affair with.

Mr. X immediately knew something is terribly wrong on an epic scale and then there was silence. Heavy breathing from both parties, each thinking to him and herself who is going to draw the first blood. Mr. X summoned up his courage and asked is everything alright darling is your mother alright. The iPad came flying and even before Mr. X could react it hit him on his balding head. And Mrs. X explodes very Mount Vesuvius like, she was screaming at him, "You bastard this, and you bastard that, you're a cheating swine, I want a divorce." Mrs. X gave a complete piece of her mind that she had kept bottled for years. Mr. X looked at the iPad and immediately fell into the same page she was in. He was caught, there was nothing to say, and Mr. X being the powerful man that he is, would not take this kind of verbal beating from his wife and the humiliation specially when both his sons where in their rooms. He knew they could hear her, so he stormed back. At the peak of his rage, he struck the coffee table, which was not from Ikea but a fancy furniture shop, told his wife she could leave if she wanted to and stormed out of the apartment.

He drove to the nearest pub which happened to be the exact same pub where I was a regular in. The time then was 6:00 pm, at that time, I was having my run, Venessa just woke up from her previous day's work and planned to go out to buy a belt for her night out with her girlfriends. Mr. X started drinking, he drank so much somewhere near mid night he was on his $12^{th}$ pint when he decided to go home. After he paid the bill, he heavily tipped the bartender who happened to be the exact same friend of mine who gave me the free pass to the club. Pleased with his tip he immediately asked Mr. X if he could do anything for him, as he saw he was clearly drunk. Mr. X said, "Help me catch a cab and tell the valet that I'll collect the car tomorrow." So, while they stood outside the pub Mr. X looks at the bartender whose name is Joy, he says, "Joy I do not want to go home do you any other place where I can go to have a good time." Joy immediately offers Mr. X his pass to Copa Cabana and tells him it is the place to be that night, this was Joy's trick to make a few extra bucks as he knew Mr. X was loaded with cash, after the tip he just gave. Joy said it was his pass to the club he purchased a week ago but due to the absence of a colleague he had to cover for him for night and couldn't go to the club. Mr. X pulled another big note from his wallet thanked Joy for the ticket and hopped into the cab.

# Chapter 2
# Girl in the Black Skirt

The taxi screeched to a halt in Copa Cabana. Mr. X stepped off the taxi and the taxi driver was relieved. Mr. X has exited the taxi as he was reeking of beer, and it was making the taxi driver nauseous off the smell. The driver took off not even bothered if there were anyone in need of his services there. The only thing that ran through his mind was to get away from Mr. X as soon as possible. As Mr. X stumbled towards the entrance of the club, the bouncers stopped and disagreed to let him in as he was already drunk. Mr. X felt belittled in front of the people standing at the entrance of the club and under the effects of the alcohol in him he went berserk like a mad man. He started to shout at the bouncers. At that exact moment my friend broke my gaze from the mysterious girl in the black skirt while I was anticipating for her to turn around, so I could get a glimpse of her face. I have been staring at her for a while now and have been telepathically asking her to turn but guess she was tuned into another frequency all together. My friend was shouting into my ears, and I was trying to understand what he was saying when I noticed one of the bouncers rushing to the DJ stand where the floor manager was standing. He spoke into his ears and the manager gestured he cannot hear anything, and the bouncer gestured back to follow him. Right at that moment a waiter was carrying drinks from the bar to the table where the mystery girl and her friends was sitting. Meanwhile Mr. X wasn't done throwing a tantrum; he was yelling, screaming and in the fit of his rage having taken enough of shit from the bouncer pushes him aside and runs into the club. He was heading straight to the mystery girl's table. The other bouncer immediately stops Mr. X right beside the mystery girl's table.

The manager tries to cut in to calm Mr. X who is still yelling and forcing his way further in, the poor waiter who was bringing the drinks got caught between them all. And in the confusion Mr. X's hand accidentally bumps into the waiter who loses his balance, and the drinks go flying right into the table where the mystery girl and her friends are sitting. The music stops, now the girls are yelling, the waiter is yelling, the bouncers are yelling, the manager is yelling, and Mr. X is yelling. All our attention turns to them and just then a spotlight fell from the heavens lighting up the mystery girl who began to turn and face us, we were sitting across them in the dance floor. While all this confusion was happening, I managed to get up and walk halfway to the girls table as I anticipated the waiter was about to drop the drinks. I have no idea why I got up to get to the girl's table. My instinct was to catch the falling drinks, guess my spider senses were activated, and I was acting out of my reflexes. But anyway, there I was halfway across the dance floor just a couple of feet from the mystery girl who now was facing me and me looking at her. I smiled as I watched her drying herself of the beer that fell on her. She looked at me and smiled and I said, "Do you and your friends want to join us?" and pointed to our table.

She said, "It's okay." I introduced myself and she said her name was Venessa. All her friends were up and have moved to the dance floor and were staring at Mr. X who have now started apologizing. "What just happened?" Venessa asked, while the manager and the bouncer who were now escorting Mr. X out of the club. I insisted Venessa and her friends to join our table while they cleaned up. She looked at me with a smile and was about to say no when Abbey one of her friends nudged her from behind. I jokingly said, "Your friend wants too," and then Venus replied, "Okay, maybe for a while."

And before anything further could be said we were joining tables and sitting together. So, I had the whole night to get to know Venessa. two rounds of tequila shots later, I asked her if she would like to go somewhere quieter so we can talk and maybe have dinner. She nodded with a smile and every time she smiled something lit up in me. We lied to the group and then headed out. I could not help but stare at how her skirt flowed down the contours of her fit body while walking out and the thoughts started coming back. I have already started to think how the night will end and was wishing to undress this fine woman who turned towards me, and I immediately switched my gaze to her lovely face. She held my hand and as we stepped out, she whispered into my ears asking if I liked what I saw. Now I knew for sure something amazing was going to happen. I joked about preferring my eyes gazing at her face than her ass. I caught a cab, and we went back to my favorite pub. Joy was joyous when he saw me come in with a fine looking woman and he immediately set us up with drinks. Venessa was becoming more and more relaxed as the night went on. Her hand was on my lap for most of the time. She kept sliding her hands on my thighs up and down while she gazed into my eyes making it seem like her hands weren't there in the first place.

Now my mind has completely shut down, I was just pretending to be listening to her while chemicals were mixing and reacting in my brain send pulses down my spine. My eyes were wandering exploring all of her and she would deliberately position herself so I can really check her out. And all this time her hand sliding up and down on my thigh. Sometimes it went a little too far and I knew for sure that she was trying to awaken the kraken. She was drunk, and the conversation started steering to an explicit nature. She whispered in my ears that she wasn't wearing any underwear and I gulped my saliva down my throat. Now I was telepathically telling the kraken not to wake up but to stay asleep. But he had a mind of his own and there was no stopping him. My erection was growing by the second and I was trying not to get a hard-on then and there in the middle of my favorite pub. Now things were getting a bit too heated, and I shifted her hand from my thigh to my knee. But no, she just would not keep her hands still. She whispered in my ears that her place is nearby and I nodded for the bill. Once the bill was paid, things were getting heated up fast. The time was around 2:30 in the morning we were in the elevator of her building and her hands now were exploring my body and mine hers as we moved up on the lift defying gravity.

Kissing began and now my hands were travelling all over her black skirt. The elevator door opens we walk into her apartment and the kissing became more passionate, she pushed me down on the couch, and I fell on the remote which turned on the TV. David Attenborough was on the Animal Planet he was saying the bull frogs had begun preparing for the mating season. Young males would have to battle many other males to prove their masculinity and the winner would get to mate as many females as he could. Dramatic music playing at the background, I have started my battle with the bra hook which seemed like a Rubik's cube, getting harder and harder to unhook. As the Bull, continued David Attenborough, having won the battle he lays on a muddy pit attracting the females by his mating calls to join him in this seasonal carnal festival. The male would mount the female in an amorous embrace famously called as the axillary am plexus. He would then fertilize the eggs as she laid them into the water. Their mating sounds could be heard throughout the mating season as they are veracious predators and aggressive horny breeders. The breeding seasons usually last for two to three months. The strong healthy males attract as many females as possible having established his territory to breed though the mating season. After he fertilizes her eggs, he releases her from his grip. Venessa and I fell on the floor breathing heavily trying to catch our breath.

As she lay on top of me breathing heavily with one hand on my chest and the other drawing circles as she traced her finger along the sides of my belly. I lay there quietly with my eyes wandering around her room, the moment after coitus with a stranger can become weird and awkward so I was thinking what next, but I didn't want to leave, I wanted more. I could also sense she wanted more because now her lips were on my chest and was moving south across my belly and this was a perfect signal that she was getting prepared for a second amorous embrace. A volcano was ready for a second time to erupt. David Attenborough continued, he was saying, deep in the African forest the Lions are preparing for their mating season, in the wild they usually breed not more than once in two years. Females are receptive to mating for three to four days within a widely variable reproductive cycle. During this time a lion generally mates for 20 to 30 minutes with up to 50 copulations in a day. Camera zooming on Lion copulating the female, confused looking Zebras running on the background. Lion falling of the lioness after his 20-minute session, Venessa let out a high-pitched moan her fingers clenched my chest and she collapsed on me. In my mind several volcanoes erupted across the planet.

The mystery girl in the black dress had thoroughly and satisfactorily rocked my world, we showered together and as I was putting on my clothes to leave the doorbell rang. I sensed a worry built up on her face and with an anxious look she asked me to keep very quiet. She looked through the keyhole and then she started panicking. Now I began to get a bit tensed not knowing what to expect. She asked me to hurry and hide under the bed. I asked her what her problem was and then she said, "Hide please, my boyfriend is here." My mind went blank I ran into the bedroom and hide below the bed. lying below the bed I didn't know what to expect. I lay still hoping he would leave soon. Then I wondered why she would do such a thing and not tell me she had a boyfriend. Thank God it wasn't her husband, but still being in this situation was a first and my heart was pounding so loud I was afraid he would hear it. Then I heard him speak he was asking her about her where bouts that night. In my head, it felt like, he knew she was banging away with me. What if he was hiding downstairs to catch us? Maybe she had her reason to cheat, and his questions made me feel like he was waiting to catch her for a while. I knew for sure that he was very suspicious.

They were sitting in the living room talking and I was paying close attention to hear what they were speaking. He wasn't happy at all as he was trying to reach her the whole night and he wanted to know why she hasn't been picking up her calls. She explained that her phone was in silent mode, and she was in a club maybe she didn't hear it. "What about when you left the club?" he enquired, she said she was too tired, and she hasn't checked any of her messages or calls yet. Then the conversation switched in Tagalog. Luckily, we showered else he would have much bigger questions to ask. I could only see their feet, walking around in the living soon. Suddenly, the conversation was taking a sweeter tone he was close to her and then her robe dropped to the floor, in my head a voice went no, no, no. *What's wrong with this guy*, I thought, *why isn't he asleep.* Then his pants fell to the floor, and they were making their way to the bedroom.

I could hear them kissing, and gently moans escaping Venessa's mouth. I couldn't believe I was in this situation and hoped he would at least leave after he was done else, I was really screwed and would have to lie under the bed until morning or whenever he left. What if he planned to stay for the next day being the weekend? God, please help me I prayed while Venessa's boyfriend started grunting like a pig. I mean he sounded so funny. I could tell he was very excited and delighted, like a kid in a candy store looking around at all the candy. With each thrust his moans were getting louder as well. He sounded like a donkey whose ass was on fire. I was trying my best no to laugh. 'Cause in between he would sound like this, "HO HO HOOOO," and then switch to "HEEEE HEEE HEEEE" with the HO's being deep voiced and the HE's being high pitched. Nothing much was heard from Venessa, and it took a great deal of strength to stop myself from laughing. I wonder what was running through Venessa's head, why wouldn't she have told me she had a boyfriend.

Two hours later I could hear the donkey snore, I slowly started to make my way out from beneath the bed. As I crept out, there lay the boyfriend naked snoring away cuddling with Venessa. I slowly made my way out of the room; I couldn't make out if she was awake as the room was pitch dark. I slowly opened the door made my way to the entrance door. When I reached the entrance door, I found out that the keys were not there. I looked around but couldn't find the keys. Not knowing what to do I started hearing sounds coming from the bedroom and immediately I went into the kitchen and hid behind the kitchen door. It was Venessa with the keys, I whispered, "In the kitchen." Venessa showed me out of her apartment and just before I left, she said she would call me and explain everything.

It was early morning; I caught a cab to my car and then drove to no particular destination as I still felt like I had to party a little more. I just didn't want to go back to my room. I hated the good times ended and I wasn't basking in the excitement of what I experienced nor was I excited that I met a wonderful, beautiful woman and the high probability of meeting her again. The sudden realization of where I was emotionally sunk in. The dark thoughts returned, and I was feeling like shit all over again. I felt I wanted to have more fun and stop feeling like shit this early in the morning that to on a Saturday. I have completely lost the ability to be happy without my secret medicines. My mind started to go back into depression, and I needed a joint to make me feel good again. I felt the pain return and I was frustrated that I didn't feel better even after last night, and the urge to keep running away from my emotions and hiding from the world came rushing back to me. I just did not want to exist as I was. This was me all the time, but I also had something that just wouldn't give up in me but in order to feel and think straight again I needed to satisfy my thirst for alcohol and smoke a joint. This new dark side of me just absolutely refused submission to anyone, to any reason and it had to get what it wanted. A voice kept telling me to keep fighting, fight through the pain, but to do that I wanted to have more fun.

I called a friend whom we call The Kite among us friends, the kite was my doctor who helped me get the medication to ease the pain. It was very early in the morning, and I knew he would be pissed if I woke him up from his sleep but there was always a possibility and plus my itch has got unbearable, he could be awake and having his last joint before he hibernated through the day. As I was driving towards his place hoping he would be up, made my urge to get high stronger by the minute. I just couldn't go home feeling depressed like this I needed to feel awesome. Finally, he picked the phone, and he was very happy to get my call and all he said was how much time do you need to get here. I replied five minutes and he disconnected. Which clearly meant the kite was high and exploring other realms and dimensions which common men do not know of. My only fear was getting there at a time where he would be too high to open the door, The Kite wouldn't know if I stood in front of him and slapped him across his face repeatedly if he zoned off to another planet.

I parked in front of his house and calmly walked to the front door and even before I could knock, the door flung open a hand darted out caught me by the collar and pulled me in and threw me on the floor. The doors shut immediately and there he stood The Kite on a high like I never seen him before and he said I just spoke to my spirit animal, he was clearly tripping on acid and he kept repeating what do you want, what do you want I'm about to go to the other side. All I wanted was weed and alcohol and he pointed me towards the table and said weed on the first drawer, second the booze is in the kitchen. Saying that he collapsed on the sofa. I could clearly make out he was in some other world talking to God knows what or who. I walked to the table in such excitement and open the first drawer and there it was my medicine. Ganja, such a divine creation, I always wondered how it even evolved and came into existence. As I was rolling myself a big thick fat joint, I wondered how the universe came up with such a creation. This plant must be made legal, I guess the universe was in a very good mood when it perceived the formula of this special plant and willed it into existence.

The kite extended his arm in anticipation that I would pass the joint, felt like he wanted me to come to just roll him one and he was getting more and more impatient. I walked over gave him the joint, lit it up, and walked straight to the kitchen to fetch the booze and I poured myself a drink and started rolling the next joint as I sipped the whisky. The Kite passed me the joint while he lit a cigarette and now, he was getting deeper into his dream world. He lay down and I started puffing on the joint, taking a sip of the whisky every now and then. It was time to play some music and I started looking for The Kite's laptop and I was getting high at the same time. With each sip of the whiskey, I felt the warm beverage warm my chest and I would sway towards drunkenness and when I puff on the joint, I would sway towards the high side or the kite side. My thoughts were shifting to calmer thoughts, and I started to emotionally disconnect with all the shit bearing emotions and was projecting to pure fucking happiness. The warmness in my heart sank deeper my muscles relaxed and I was swept away into pure ecstasy. The weed was strong, and it started taking its effect.

I was stepping into a dream world feeling light, my heart filled with so much joy. I was walking in circles between the sitting room and kitchen looking for the laptop. Though in my mind I knew I was looking for something I reached a good high that kept me in a state of amnesia. I forgot what I was looking for and then I had to concentrate harder to bring myself out of the light headedness to remember what I was looking for. Ah, yes, the laptop and then I would have reached the kitchen looked around and returned to the sitting room forgetting what it was I was looking for and when I reached the sitting room think again and remember it was the laptop and wouldn't find it there in the sitting room and return to the kitchen to look for it again. This happened a couple of times and it felt like an hour has passed by, because I was fighting the high to stay focused but would forget when I gave in to the high. I badly wanted to stay high, and I wanted to play the music too. So, I had to decide, and concentrated to find the laptop. Which I eventually found in the bedroom. In the bedroom I was welcomed to a wonderful sight, two hookers, I hate calling them that so let's call them pros, short for professionals, were lying naked on the bed asleep with their asses faced up.

Immediately I forgot what I was looking for again and completely forgot about the music cause now I was alerted to the gorgeous round asses looking back at me. I shouted back at the Kite asking him if he still remembers he's got two beautiful professionals lying on his bed. The kite in his own spiritual plane talking to angels from other dimensions completely forgot about them. Then I remembered again, yes, the music, because I just wanted to sit down at this point, smoke more weed, listen to some good music, drink more whiskey, and then later join the pros. I looked around the room finally found the laptop got it back to the sitting room sat down plugged it to the speakers and finally got to play some music, took like forever to just get the laptop and I was exhausted looking for it, felt like an hour passed, just for the sake of some good songs. I was feeling more and more anxious wondering if my high, which I was experiencing would end, and I would have missed the opportunity to chill like I wanted to chill. Because finding the laptop seemed like an eternity and now choosing the right song felt exhausting and so I just played the usual playlist.

Once when the music played, I immediately looked at the watched and found it has been only 20 mins since the whole ordeal. Which felt like hours for me, finally sitting on the couch relaxed sipping on the whiskey I lit the second joint. Vibrations everywhere the music was taking me to my dream world. I began shedding all the heavy emotions and was getting lighter and lighter until my body ceased to exist. I felt like pure energy, just vibrations moving melodiously around the room. My body began to be absorbed into the sofa like water being absorbed into a sponge. I was finally free; I could feel electrical charges fire in my brain and lighting up my spinal cord. I was in peace I could feel my soul come alive, a sudden urge to conquer the world started burning in me. I felt alive, I felt like me, reborn standing strong and tall, I could accomplish anything I wanted. Why can't I feel like this all the time, this is how I wanted to feel when I am sober. I could see every insidious program in me that blocked my progress and asked my sub-conscious to delete them. I knew who I was, what I wanted and how to achieve them. While I allowed every part of me to drown in this pool of divine like energy, I wished and prayed my life would be different, I hope that I will be saved from this depression.

Just when I thought that the pros were up and were standing naked in front of me, I didn't even realize it until I had tits appear mysterious through the smoke right up to my face. I was too high to ask for their names so let's called them Blue and Brown. Blue had deep blue eyes and they were glowing in the poorly lit smoky room. Brown had beautiful brown hair that seemed to be floating around like she was submerged in water. Blue crouched in front me and took the joint of my hand and brown took my whiskey. She drank the remaining of the glass and refilled my drink and handed me the glass. The joint was being passed around and the three of us were sitting on the couch introducing each other, I just remembered them as blue and brown. I started to roll the next joint when Blue asked me to open the third drawer and there lay some magic shrooms. I just wanted the weed, so I handed her the mushrooms. Brown ran to the kitchen and came back with honey and the girls dipped the mushrooms in the honey and ate them. They lay there relaxed waiting for the shrooms to kick. Blue kept insisting me to try the shrooms, but I was happy with the weed.

I lit, my third joint and then gulped a mouth full of whiskey. Sandwiched between two beautiful naked women the relaxation drifted into a whole new level. I got a bit too drunk and so I puffed on just the weed to take the edge of the alcohol so I can switch back to the high from the weed. I felt like my body was merging with the girl's bodies and the vibrations started to merge us all together as one giant ball of energy. Felt like I was flowing like water from side to side in the form of waves. It was dead calm, aroused on having these beautiful women beside me. The energies seemed to be peaking to a whole new level this time. Sensations of being trapped between soft warm bodies on either side filled my body with a new feeling of calmness, mixed with joy, bliss and ecstasy, the emotion felt like an orgasm taking different forms of emotions intertwining with one another. They were mixing and re-mixing in ways unexplainable. The music kept blowing me away to deeper stages of relaxation and deeper sensations as my imagination went completely wild. It was a complete orgy of just energies mixing into a blissful cocktail.

I came to learn Blue was a Psychology major and Brown had a kid back in her country who she supported from her job as an escort. Each of them had a tale of trauma which led them to take this path. I realized all of us were lost souls trying to reconnect with our source trying to find our way back. We all needed this freedom that we could experience without judgement or control far away from this harsh, brutal world. All we wanted was to be free, free from our own self destruction and free from the world that was self-destructing itself. My thoughts began to wander on its own, I wondered how simple we all were in our truest form yet so unique and creatively diverse wonderful beings we were, but how complicated it became once we entered the world. We are forced to wear different masks to fit in, and further reduce ourselves to become a certain kind of a person, who we are not inside. The real world felt so fake and a fabrication of an idea we are forced to live in to survive. An idea fed by powerful people who wants to keep us controlled so we keep them rich and powerful. But there also exists a few people who lights the path to the mystical side of this planet, awakened people, who walk among us having lifted this illusion away and live outside any of this mind control, they have set themselves free. And I so badly wished to be like them. To live in my own terms, creating my own success and sharing it with the ones that need help. Guess the weed is working as the philosophies are flowing out of me.

    I wondered what Venessa would be up to now. I wondered what part she had to play in my life. I knew she wasn't the one, because I no longer wanted a relationship. I just wanted to fly solo for now, on my own, and get to understand the real me, the real authentic me before the programming was done upon me from childhood, maybe I want to be this person first and then decide about marriage later. I remembered her beautiful smile her laugh and the night I spent with her. I now felt a connection to her which I knew will go away once I'm sober. The mystery girl in the black dress was put on my path to teach me something I thought. As I puffed deeper and held the smoke in, I felt a thousand fires come to life in my brain. I yearned for adventure, I longed for each day to feel new and exciting. The kite was drifting deeper into his fantasy world. Brown persuaded him to the bedroom, and she carried him into the bedroom. Kite looked at me with a grin just before he entered the bedroom and said enjoy and disappeared into the room. It felt like he vanished into the mist made from all the smoke, and the room was filled with smoke.

I wondered what constituted the fundamentals of becoming a successful person. Does, character got to do with it, does your personality, hardworking nature, is it persistence or is it your capability to transmute to higher states of consciousness so you draw the experience to you. I know many hard-working people with exemplary character/personality but aren't at all successful. And I am sure there are gurus and monks who live frugal lives not quit living the comfortable life. Then what is it, what is the formula or the secret. Is it all the above or are only selected individuals whose destiny has been specially written by the Supreme Consciousness allowed to achieve such feats in life? And why are most of these people such major assholes. I know some nice folks who are very honest, sincere, and hardworking people and they are gems, I mean absolute gems I would say, but they live miserable lives. What is the mystery behind this, there are volumes of books written on this? Most of it revolves around the same principles but then why isn't there a breakthrough of let's say at least 30% of the world's population reaching that level of success. Or is it that only 1% have that in them to achieve the level of success that seems so impressive. Maybe they are withholding the key factors or secrets they have discovered to amass such results in their lives. I wonder where I am in this spectrum. What should I be doing to get the hell out of where I am to flying high among the miracle workers? What am I missing? What am I not paying attention to?

I wonder what God looks like, is he an old man sitting in a room filled with stacks and stacks of papers and a typewriter sitting at a quiet corner writing people's destiny. Or is he an old man working in a workshop sculpting everyone by hand

and then programming their destiny into their DNA. Is he a monk sitting under the eternal holy tree of the cosmos in meditation and creating everything and everyone we know of by his thoughts? Is he listening to me right this instant? Did he put all these doubts in my head? Maybe somewhere among the stacks of papers my destiny would be lying in a file having the same thought typed out. But for now, I feel he is a prankster who loves to put me in situations that is driving me nuts and that to in a time I generally feel like shit, I bet he's getting a kick out of it while he typed this chapter of my life out. I mean with the shit luck I'm having you'd agree that he is a prankster. Can you believe Donald Trump became the President of the self-proclaimed greatest country in the world, USA? Will you allow an Engineer to be a doctor and perform a surgery on you? No right? But why is that wrong with allowing it? Don't worry you don't have to answer that it is obvious that an Engineer hasn't been through medical school for one, and secondly, he has no experience to conduct a diagnosis due to the lack of medical knowledge and simply because he's a fucking Engineer. Now what qualification should a candidate whose running for President have, why is the most important job always taken up by completely unqualified people. How is that we end up voting for them. Politics is just clean bullshit, I always felt politics is the art to fool people by men who is greedy for power and money.

I'm not saying all of them is bad, but if you do check the majority is inclining towards bull shitty side. What were the odds of Donald Trump winning, was this part of God's plan or is this man so brilliant to fool the public to gain their trust and then become president? Imagine it, he came out of nowhere and wins the elections the rest of the candidates should has spent years of their life in politics climbing the political ladder accumulating the necessary experience and then aiming to become the president. But this guy an Engineer, metaphorically speaking, in a doctor's disguise managed to convince not one but the majority of the people in the country that he is an expert Doctor even when everyone knew he was an Engineer and then he managed to convince them expertly to actually win. Hold on I know he wasn't and Engineer, I'm just using the Engineer, Doctor analogy to explain how a completely unqualified man was given the job, how did he pull this off, I mean why is it that the real ones who deserve it are under looked and ignored. What strange magic does Donald trump know off? My mind is blown away by people like him. It pisses me off to the moon and back, but I cannot stop to wonder, how do they do it? Makes the rest of us look like complete idiots.

    I heard and then saw fingers snapping right in front of my face, it was Blue her eyes glowing bright through the smoke snapped me out of my deep thoughts. She was shaking her head with an expression that read, "Where are you dude, I'm sitting right here butt naked. Do something." I smiled back grabbed the joint from her hand and took a deep puff. She smiled back while she got up and put on a T-shirt and then came back and sat close to me. She put my arm around her while we smoked and kept passing the joint. We ended up watching a movie, I don't remember what we were watching but I was beginning to feel hungry and accidentally ate a couple of shrooms which was kept next to the packet of chips. I wasn't even aware that I consumed them as I was deep in the movie. About 20 mins into the movie rainbows started shooting out of the laptop screen and were hitting me on my forehead and I couldn't believe what was happening, but it felt strange but in a good and soothing way. Felt like the universe was helping me download information from the laptop. A couple of minutes later the brightness of the laptop increased like an angel was about to step off the laptop screen which began to look more and more like a door of light. I looked at blue, her face looked like she had giant blue colored headlight shaped eyes and each time she blinked the color would go black and then back to blue. I couldn't figure out what was happening, and I felt like I needed some water, and I couldn't get up as my feet had disappeared into the floor. I felt stuck to the ground as I stood up, I felt like I was a giant towering very high over the floor. I could have easily been like a hundred feet, and I looked down on my foot as it narrowed down a long way to my ankles and my feet disappearing into the floor. I sat down in disbelief wondering what was happening, am I experiencing an awakening I thought to myself. Meanwhile Blue was watching me and laughing and then I started laughing looking at her in disbelief of what was happening. She asked me to sit down and relax and enjoy the trip.

When I sat down my body burst into a million butterflies and flew across the room in a circle. It looked like a small tornado of butterflies right there in the sitting room. I was the million butterflies, I was the tornado and suddenly nothing, I vanished into the ceiling. I was clueless what was happening I never had an experience like this before. No type of weed gave be hallucinations, it must be super weed I thought to myself. Having not figured out that it was the effect of the shrooms I took, I no longer knew if I was awake or daydreaming or sleep dreaming. I knew whatever was happening to me and around me and it felt like I was consciously everywhere, but I wasn't sure. I began to think am I sleeping, and it became confusing. Because I was as awake as awake could be but I couldn't see myself anywhere so I must be sleeping and dreaming this right. Right? I thought to myself, this trip seemed like it was going on forever. A bright light appeared before me, out of the nothingness appeared Blue but she had wings like a dragonfly and her blue eyes shining bright as the sky. Felt like she was seeing through me, and she leaned forward and kissed me. her lips were so soft, and electric, felt a strange blissful wave of energy flow through me. she was soft, never felt a body that soft before in my life, each time she kissed I felt ripples of the same electric sensation flow through out my body. The energy would explode on my lips and moving through reach cell in my body in the form of waves. Blue unbuttoned my shirt and wherever she touched me I felt the same sensation run through my body.

Her body seemed to be made of light and each touch felt like pleasure I cannot describe how good it felt. And when I touched her, she would change color, her body would turn into a bright yellow light from a bright white light. *Maybe this is how it felt for the Gods when they engaged in sex,* I thought. I felt her, the colors from her body flow on my skin and I began to appear again. I could feel the colors flow on my skin, felt like feathers were being brushed gently but all over my body. Now the energies were flowing in various directions with several epicenters and their energies colliding and mixing with each other and waves of energies where also flowing from my body into Blue's and vice versa. A warm intense sensual sensation exploded as our torsos were locked in union. Bright orange light shot out of our torsos and it felt wet and warm fluids flowed down on the sides of my hip. As she rocked and placed her hands on my chest, her fingers disappeared into my skin. I felt light flow through her fingers into my heart and instantaneous the warm wetness flowing over my hips I felt like I was about to explode. So much energy was being transferred into my body from hers. The sensations building in my body felt bigger than an any orgasm experienced before. It was indescribable, her soft moans where getting louder and it seemed to echo around the room. The sound of her moans started to build and with each moan a greater intense erotic vibe would sweep through me. The sounds seemed to be echoing into a thousand echoes. Versions of both of us started to project out like a frame and each frame would be the moment that originated from the moan that escaped from blue's mouth. As she grinded and gyrated on me and moaned, a frame would pop out with us in that moment of the moan and each frame would arrange itself frame by frame side by side above us. Each frame would have our motion up to the moan in that moment of the moan and with all the frames arranged side by side would be the continuous reality happening between me and Blue on that coach. Imagine the moans of all the frames happening in their moans in time causing echoes in echoes. The built up in energy was exponential, I felt like a nuclear bomb ticking down for a massive explosion and all I could hear was her moan and the thousand echoes of echoes of moans from each frame. I could feel her touch and all the touches from each moment of the frames per moan. I could feel the tremendous heat dissipate from her wetness drip over my waist. I could see her flip her hair backwards and feeling her press her hips deeper and arching her back more as her head leaned backwards letting out louder and louder moans.

There were like a thousand frames now each flickering like a count down and when each flickered out it would merge with the previous frame and so forth. I began to feel that due to my body heat I began turning into vapor and Blue seemed like turning into water. And with one big moans Blue turned completely into water and I was complete vapor. We were engulfed in a giant ball of light which contained all the energy within and as the energy settled our bodies manifested back to its form and there, she laid above me her arms tightly wrapped around me calming from the storm she brought upon me she twitched randomly letting out quiet moans. Our breathing was in union, and we were calming down. Felt like we were lying naked on a meadow that stretched forever and the warm sun was shining on us.

Watching the sky, a couple of feet above me, I knew I was still high and might be dreaming all of this. And then everything went dark for a while. I began to hear voices in the far distance, it wasn't clear, but I knew they were calling out to me. The voice got louder and louder and then I woke up, The Kite woke me up, I got up and dressed and realized I wasn't dreaming about what happened. Blue was not to be seen anywhere around. It was 4:00 in the evening, and I was starving, the kite rolled a joint and asked me to take a shower, he said, "We are going out." After my shower we smoked the joint rolled another for the road. The plan was to go to the pub and have a couple of drinks and finally eat something. On the way he enquired, "So how was it?" "Which part?" I asked back. He was enquiring about Blue, but I replied saying the weed was tight, never tripped like that before. The Kite burst into laughter, Blue told him that I accidentally had the shrooms thinking it was chips and gave her the performance of a lifetime. The Kite tapped my shoulder and told me about my accidental consumption of the shrooms which resulted in epic sex with Blue, and that was a story enough for him to tell for a year to whoever he met.

We arrived at the pub and couple of beers down I told the Kite about Venessa and the night I had with her, he burst out in laughter again after hearing I was under the bed when her boyfriend did the nooky with her. I ended up inviting her as the Kite wouldn't stop asking me to invite her over, and she came, the three of us sat and drank. The Kite and Venessa hit it off immediately, I began to feel strange, The Kite was flirting with her, and she was flirting back. I began to slowly fall in the background. I couldn't believe it was happening right in front of me. She did not have her hand on me this time. But I noticed her face brighten up with her eyes wide open and she was laughing at everything he said. I was wondering what was happening. In my mind I was thinking what about me, what about all the stuff you told me last night. Wait what's going on here, maybe I'm still high or I'm sleeping. Wake up, wake up I kept saying to myself. I excused myself and went to the washroom and when I came back Venessa was sitting beside The Kite now. I began to think maybe they know each other, and all this was a prank. But noooo, they were like two children playing on the beach building sandcastles. I had enough of it and told them I had to go and took off. I was expecting Venessa to say something but no all she said was okay carry on.

Pissed off and angry I kept all the weed and shrooms the kite left back in the car. On my way back to my room. I began to feel sad and rejected. I did meet Venessa a couple of times after that, but everything changed and now she just wanted me as a friend. And to make matters worse you won't believe it The Kite ended up marrying Venessa six months later. Yes, I know your shocked, when they broke the news to me, I felt the sucker punch to my gonads by the universe once again, successfully. My shit luck did not stop there it epically grew to epic heights but more on that later.

So, The Mystery girl in the back skirt ended up with The Kite, imagine the steps the universe took for her to end up with The Kite. Like Mr. X, I too was just a pawn played around by the universe. Wonder what Donald Trump would have done if he was me. Maybe he would have refused to hide under the bed, oh God I'm pathetic. He must have bullied her boyfriend to submission and had him hide under the bed while he was rocking the bed with Venessa. I wonder what he would have done with The Kite. Anyway, I had enough of the universe using me as a pawn to make other people more money, find love, be their safety net, and basically be a punching bag. Enough was enough, I am putting my foot down here, I'm drawing the line. I challenge the universe, suddenly a flash of light went off in front of me. That was a speeding camera, again, and I just got a speeding fine. Rest of the trip back to my place was quiet but I did light that joint and smoke it, but quietly feeling sad and rejected.

# Chapter 3
# Father, Oh Father, Where Art Thou?

I have witnessed what I believe is the greatest love story there ever was. The story of my father and mother. It is a tragic one but can't deny it was a great one. There are no perfect love stories in real life. But only in fairy tales or fiction novels, real love makes you bleed. Real love is pain, its sacrifice, its acceptance, its forgiveness and sometimes it is sort of a suicide. Do emotions exist only in us humans. Do the birds, animals and the trees feel them too? Do they love? My father to me was a complete mystery and one of my biggest regrets was not getting to know him more, to understand him. Strange how love keeps you locked and trapped in a relationship that feels like fire. Sometimes I even wondered if what they had was love. Marriage does that to people, it drives the two to the point of insanity and yet they just cannot part from one another. Only death's sweet release can take them apart and until then they would bleed within themselves to love one another trapped in each other's hearts. My mother was a sweet soul that knew only to nurture. She only knew to love and fix anything broken with her love. Her kindness goes deep, a gentle woman who cooks with her heart and like superglue keeps the family close.

I not going to start their story from the beginning, I'll begin when a darkness so dark crept into our lives, its claws so evil it devoured soul's whole. It turned righteous great men to monsters without warning and made them their puppet to destroy their homes. They are bottled and potent consumed for fun at nights but if it gets to you, you'll be trapped in its clutches devouring your mind. It's sold like water legal everywhere, so many great men have fallen prey, so many families have been destroyed to dust by its influence. Once when your addicted it turns you against yourself you fight with your loved ones, and makes it seem like you love to hurt them, while you end up dissolving in its influence painfully. Killing you slowly giving you time to do your damage. It makes you play wicked dirty emotional games to suffocate the joy and suck the life of everything driving you insane. It comes quietly making you feel good at first and once when you fall in its death trap you cannot live without it, and it sticks with you like a curse. It is a sad love story of such a couple who died a thousand deaths when they lived together and a thousand deaths after he was gone.

Are the lives of people who are prone to destruction written by the almighty or is the individual to blame for falling into an addiction? Dark shadows crept around in the house at nights, it wasn't safe to stay out of your bedroom cause if you were caught by the monster, it was torture that night. Like the beast in Beauty and the Beast, my father was once a handsome prince loved by everyone, who came into his existence. He was bold, confident, and intelligent a genius of another kind. His personality was like gravity, watching him was a magnificent sight. A young surgeon whose brilliance was known far and wide. A jovial fellow, king of one liners, my best friend who gave me this life. Born to a family with super riches, youngest to several brothers and sisters. He was a star on the making showing a lot of promise right from his childhood days. Everyone knew how special he was, everyone loved him for what he was many desired to be like him because he was fun and a loving playful man. He mingled with the young ones and stood respected with the elders of the family.

Like my mother he was a kind man, who would help anyone who wanted his help. A leader a star that shined so bright, my father was my superman he was my light. He had a big heart, and he gave every bit of himself to the people around him. He was a family man who loved his family, but the young prince had problems growing up. Somewhere along his journey he was introduced to the demons that would eventually turn his life to dust. Rumors float around and I'm not going to point fingers, let the guilty ones who misled him be brought to justice in nature's own way. He rebelled and fought among his siblings, he made it difficult for them, I bet he gave them hell making it impossible for them to handle him, having lost his father at a young age he was at the mercy of his mother and his siblings who were caught up in their own lives, and this little prince was left to his mind. His rebellion grew louder and harder to control, years of being difficult and flowing against the tide made it difficult for his family to control him and he made it impossible for them to help him at times, as the years went by and his siblings grew impatient, they could not any longer put up with him, to them he seemed broken, broken he was in a way nobody understood him, sometimes I wonder if he knew that about himself. They waited and hoped he would change his life but also secretly met and plotted against him. The prince now a man married with a wife, she gave him a son and sweet little baby girl child.

Though he was a man now there was an unloved boy within him, who missed his father and wanted love and attention. He was sacred and afraid being the youngest one, all he had was his mother and siblings to protect him and guide him through his tantrums. Maybe he felt lonely and abandoned inside, the truth nobody will ever know because he never discussed it with anyone, not even his wife. Many years since came a faithful night the young prince had to face destiny's cruel plan that was set in motion from the skies, familiar faces met and talked, and they were troubled by his dog they were stressed over by the damaged it has caused. Having had enough of this man who felt like a curse and enough grief they had, words were thrown at him in the fit of anger and the fight began, which felt like it lasted a life time that fateful night. They banished him from the palace and into exile they wanted him immediately out of their sight.

For a reason so trivial embarrassing to tell the judgement was given I guess this was destiny's test. To this day everybody regrets it, they wished they could have done it different, but the young prince was to stubborn and hard to handle. The cops came and enquired but he did not perspire and handled them with zest, but the drama escalated from then. They all grouped, and the verbal war began, accusations were thrown around and the judgement was read. Tears fell that night from my mother's eyes she too was accused that faithful night. The Gods were watching from the heavens above and I bet that they too were crying cause this situation seemed unjust, but it was one of his many life's trials. With a heavy heart the young prince packed his belongings and left and with him came his wife and children, with no place to go too, no place to rest. What broke that day was my father's heart, it broke to the extent that none of us to this day understands or will ever fathom because the years that came after were only dark. I always wondered why it happened like this on that sad day maybe this was what the heavens planned for him, so he'd learn to change and make hay.

As the young prince left his big palace the news spread in town and his arrival was closely anticipated. He found a small place for his family, and they settled in well nearby his cousin's house. The news reached the demons and they rejoiced at his arrival; they knew he was vulnerable, so they visited him every night in the form of a liquid to relieve the pain he carried inside. At the start life was so good, he kept drinking but there was no abuse. The sadness in him ran to deep, it fractured his soul and broke him completely. He cried in dark corners late at night drinking and drinking hoping he'll get all right. Slowly the sadness turned to hate and from that hate came anger. The anger in him fueled the drinking this affected his work and the demons kept winning. What was an activity that was partaken only at the night, couldn't keep him happy so the drinking began eventually at broad day light. The hospitals could not function without him, his bosses knew how good he was at his job and was in a dilemma to fire or keep him. But the anger bubble burst and turned to rage the monsters now had more control over him we were beginning to lose him at this stage.

My mother cried and begged him to stop at this time, she began to fight with him to save him from his mad vice. They argued and fought, he shouted, and she screamed, but my mother's message was lost in the breeze. He grew worse and was ticking like a bomb never knew when he would burst to scream and shout. My sister hid in her room terrified; something was happening to my father she thought quietly sobbing hoping he won't hear her cries. The demon has won the first battle he got his claws deep in him, who was quietly breaking him apart from within. The pain he was in was very evident and it seemed like there was no other cure than alcohol as his medicine. My sister was sacred of her father she did not know what mood he would be in, so she hid in her room after school every evening. What was once a happy family was now a distant memory with hope my mother fought for his wellbeing everyday not knowing that nightmare was just beginning, then his addiction took the form of a snake that was growing bigger and bigger day by day, the harder he defended the snake the bigger it got, strangling and swallowing anything in its path.

He was there somewhere deep inside, but he noticed someone else emerging from his mind. He was scared for his family and some days he would come back to us as his original self-bringing the laughter and making promises that the worst has been put to rest. At this stage we would go on for days as a happy family. But who are we kidding, can a broken heart heal so easily? My mother prayed and prayed to her Gods, but they were deaf to her prayers. It was the Devil's time, and he came prowling to victimize. The changes were evident and when things just got better, he would relapse and plunge deeper into his liquor. At this stage people noticed the bright prince was falling. While he stumbled in barely able to stand each night into his apartment. He would scream and shout at his wife signs of physical abuse were beginning to gleam through his eyes. He controlled as much as he could at his early stages, and he loved his wife dearly through all these ages. He woke up every morning apologizing to his wife asking her forgiveness and promising her he will change and stop the drinking since last night. He told her softly and held her close, as he loved her deeply and couldn't figure why he was falling out of control. My mother believed in him and assured him it was all right. She says she prays for him to the Gods to save him and bring him to the light. "I believe in you my love she whispered in his ears, I feel your pain, but drinking is not going to solve your problems so wake up before it's too late. You were once a brilliant man, and you still are him so please don't forget that. I'd walk with you no matter what and believe in you so be strong. Let's not worry about the past and let's begin today renewed and be free from the past."

This was a routine every morning, sort of a ritual it was so he could find the strength to change for the good. But so devious and insidious are the devil's plans the promises he made in the morning would be broken and he'd come back drunk again in the evening mad, mad he was because he couldn't keep the promises. "Yes, Bitch, he would say I drank let all of this go to ruins." He couldn't stand her during the nights because it was killing him, he could not keep those promises and couldn't understand why, and this tortured him. He loved her dearly this I knew but he'll hurt her in the evenings while he drank like a mule. My sister hid quietly in her room growing anxious day by day wondering when she will be rescued. She missed her father, who played with her, who took her out for ice cream and bought her dolls and teddy bears with fur. She missed her father who made her laugh, who carried her on his shoulder and carried her in his arms. Quietly she sat with her imaginary friends making tea for her dolls and teddy her stuffed bear. Pretending to be a princess in her dream land talking to her imaginary friends about her prince who'll come to rescue her from this hell.

The snake grew bigger and thickened in girth it lay beside my father and it would hiss and whisper into his hurting heart. "Drink my king, drink," it whispered and hissed whenever my mother tried to stop him it strangled her and bite. It screamed at her your husbands mine don't try to save him or I'll eat you alive. It stood tall at 12 feet could be easily around 100 feet, scary and wicked were its hisses. It sends chills of fear down our spines, so we hid under the beds out of its sight. Scared and petrified we wondered where it came from, while Father sat on the couch unaware drinking his rum. It controlled him and took over his mind. Poisoning his soul and swallowing his spirit it made my father its puppet. Whispering evil thoughts into his mind strengthening his pain and the drinking multiplied. It trapped us in our small, cramped apartment and threatened to kill us if we called out for help. It followed my father everywhere and kept a close watch on Mother, keeping her scared.

Trapped in a reality with no light and the curtains drawn shut, so the truth dare escape from that apartment and the giant snake slithered around and made sure we obeyed its needs. A devious game was at play, the demons that lurked once in the shadows have now manifested into a giant snake that controlled my father. He was like a zombie; we have completely lost him at this time. I knew I was looking at my father, but he was no longer the man who he used to be. My mother was helpless and felt trapped, she pretended to be fine around friends and family. The snake was clever to keep my father behaved during gathering and kept a very close eye on Mother. Every night she was mentally abused, it cursed and screamed at my mother. It told her, she was no good and a failure as a wife, she was useless to be a mother, she lost hope when it threatened it can decide to hurt her kids at any time and she wouldn't be able to do anything because she was a helpless bitch. My mother prayed and prayed hoping for a miracle to walk through the door and save her from this disgrace. She was humiliated and hurt from the torture she sat silently looking at her love who seemed not to be bothered while he seemed lost in his own world drinking away his pain.

She wondered what happened to her husband, what must she do to save him from that beast. She asked for the Gods for strength and decided to slay the snake and free her husband from its influence. Having not worked for months and spending heavily on his drink's money was beginning to be an issue for the prince. So, he borrowed money from his cousins who used this opportunity to get his help and they paid for his alcohol as well.

Eventually, his cousins too abandoned him. He was drinking too much on business trips and they could not control him from his drinking quests. Guilty for buying the liquor they stopped contacting him, his dirty secret was exposed, and the news spread. Several attempts were made several of his cousins came, interventions and interventions later they all gave up. They all met the snake terrified of it they ran away. Now my mother was completely alone to face its wrath. She was relieved when they all came but the snake was too mighty for all of them to face. It hissed and screamed bloody murder and they cowered before its wrath and hurled. The darkness was too much for them to bear and with heavy hearts they left despaired. My mother summoned all her courage, and an epic battle was fought, and blood was spilt. And finally, the snake was taken out and my father emerged from it.

We all embraced as a family my father was back and we were happy. My weary mother held his hand she said let's get away from here to another land. Let's start over in another place lets us forget all this hate and the pain. As he moved to work in the next city, he earned well and made us happy. My sister was happy she got her father back he then noticed he's missed five years of her life while he was lost being a drunk which made him sad. She was now a young woman in her tweens, and he wondered where he was, and the past felt like a bad dream. But the devil played another hand and his destiny turned again to more mishap. From the shadows emerged Mr. Hyde and possessed my father one fine night, the pain that slept awakened and the horrors of hell broke loose in this head. Lonely in another city without my mother beside him, he woke up sweating one horrified night. Waking up with a thirst he couldn't explain like a vampire lusting for blood alcohol he reclaimed, and the liquid turned him forever into Hyde who would eventually drive him insane.

A new beast was born stronger than before, he lay low in the darkness devouring bottle after bottle. Madness filled his mind; a new insanity was born within him. Meanwhile back home my mother awaited my return, I was in boarding school coming home for the summer vacation. Clueless about the events that unfolded with my father, my mother called him he was unreachable that night, maybe he's asleep son she said we will visit him tomorrow and spend the holidays by his side.

Excited to meet him we all packed, my mother shouted put the Walkman away and help me with the bags. Little did we know of the storm that was forming, a dark cloud gathered with the thunder roaring. The lights went off a chill went down my spine. Mother said it's nothing just bad weather outside. My sister went to bed excited about the trip and my mother making last minute arrangements. I felt sick to my stomach a fear in me grew the weather seemed like a bad omen, but I was hoping it wasn't true. I had a hunch that something was wrong, but I couldn't tell what it was.

Next day we set of on our journey it rained like the heavens were warning us and wanted us to stay back but Mother insisted we carry on with the journey as my father was alone in another city. My fears grew stronger as we drove, the chauffeur looked at me because I was sitting there looking like I've seen a ghost. He tapped on my shoulders and said it's alright, it's just bad weather and we'll be alright. Little did he know what bothered me, for I had a very ill feeling filling me. The skies roared with thunder and lightning strikes felt like we were driving to hell and only I could see through this illusion in my mind. And trust me I saw the devil stand on the roadside staring at me with a scary smile, the lightning lit up his face and his crooked smile, his smile spooked me while the rain poured heavily distorting his face. It happened in a second, I saw him, he smiled clearly under the lightning's light. I turned towards my mother to tell her, but the moment happened so fast I just kept it to myself knowing we were doomed forever. My instincts told me something bad was going to unfold I wished I was wrong, but the fear has already taken its hold.

We arrived at 6:00 pm. It was a small town; dark clouds filled the skies seemed like more rain was forecasted for the night. The air was cool, and ground was muddy, thick green overgrown bushes on either side of a long and narrow road finally ended at a big gate and beyond the gate was an old bungalow. It was quiet, the silence was so annoying I felt a strange ringing in my ears. The keys were kept in a flowerpot near the main door. We went inside and settled down; Father was at the hospital doing his rounds. It was cold inside the bungalow, the air felt moist from all the rain, it began to drizzle, thin waves of mist flowed in from all direction, and then it was pitch dark and night fell. We could hardly see anything because of the thick mist which crept into the bungalow from beneath the main door. There were moths everywhere of all kinds flying around annoying my sister. My mother couldn't reach my father, she called him several times on the phone but there was no reply.

The silence broke by the sound of a car approaching from a distance. We could see the head lights appearing through the mist. I was filled with mixed emotions not knowing what to expect, my heart was racing wondering if everything will be alright. The car came to a halt in the porch, and out stepped my father with a smile. I was so relieved to see him sober and in a great mood. We talked and laughed the whole night. My father was in best of his spirit that night. We were a joyous family that night. We went out as a family after a very long time, we had dinner and he took us for a drive. There was so much laughter that night all our hearts were overwhelmed with joy, finally it felt my father was back for good. He is so amazing and fun to hang around when he's sober. It was hard to stay away from him, he would keep cracking jokes and we would laugh until our stomachs hurt. I remember sitting, with the family all on the veranda, sitting together looking at fireflies, joking and laughing.

The next twenty days with him was so magical. I completely forgot about the bad omens and all the horrible sights, it felt like we were in heaven. Somewhere in between our stay he did start drinking again but it was under a control, and he was fun to hang around with. At the end of our stay there my father too came along with us back home. He had got another job back in our home city and things were beginning to look bright and promising. Little did we know it was Hyde's plan all along. Once we reached the city and he started work in his new hospital, chaos broke loose, this would be the start of completely losing my father as a man to alcohol for a second time. This time there was no recovery those 20 days was the last happy memories we had as a family. He would never be the same again, he had completely become Mr. Hyde, the level of mental abuse my mother been through was in a whole new level, this is when the physical abuse began. The beating stopped after the day I was big enough to defend her, but the mental abuse kept growing as years passed by. Felt we were trapped in hell and escaping seemed like an impossible option. The level of stress, pain and the fighting reached exhausting levels. I wonder to this day how we made it out of it all keeping our sanity. If it wasn't for my mother, we would have wound up dead somewhere.

Father oh Father where art thou
Have you forsaken us; can we be a family now?
Who is this pretender in your shoes, is he the devil because it doesn't feel like you?

Strangling the life out of us one by one
If you are somewhere out there, please come and save us.
We are bleeding inside, our bones cracking
Ours organs constricting, blood squirting
Emotionally drained, hyper ventilating.
The snake might be gone but Mr. Hyde is winning
Fear reaching unnatural levels
Feels like I'm about to pop a blood vessel
The monster is out loose coming to abuse, feels like I'm half asleep hitting the snooze
Says he is going to get his gun
Says he wants to fire some bullets for some recreational fun
Can you see us, Dad, do you feel our pain?
Can you hear us or are our screams going in vain?
Suffocated and frustrated, we stay stuck between these walls
Hoping one day you'll break free and save us all
I had enough, just kill us now, get that knife and let's end this now
You're playing Dr. Jekyll and Mr. Hyde
Playing your cruel mind games calling me a swine
Shouting and screaming while you give Mother a beating
The poor thing still loves you watching her sad life in a loop repeating
Lurking and lingering around our rooms making sure we are petrified and doomed
You stay up drinking all through the night, threatening us of our lives
Then you wake up in the morning sobbing, sad and apologizing
This dangerous loop we live in, is this the life you want us to be in.

To deaths open arms we march together, hoping that in death at least we be happy together
Father oh Father where art thou
I'm breaking, falling piece by piece, Mother is completely broken now it's up to me
You give and then you take
You love and then you hate
We had enough of your meaningless games
I fear one day Mother might kill herself, because this misery she cannot take
What happened to you, you were once great
You were once my best friend and now we only hate
What happened oh Father, why did we turn out like this
Wasn't there any other way for us to be together and live
You say I must stay strong while you drink and drink and blame me for all the wrongs
I hoped and wished you would change; these were the only reasons I shouted back and fought out in rage
I just wanted my father, not the drunk fuck who embarrassed us in front of others
Despite it all I still got you
I felt your pain and hate and understood you
I stood by you and had your back never thought you'll grow to hate me and curse me for this and that
You left me with no choice, and I hated myself for it
Fighting with you was the last thing I wanted
Fate is a painful deceiver playing its own games
We should have stood together instead but everything went in vain
We tore each other apart and hurt each other well
And in the end, I lost you forever to death

I wish I could turn back time to change our story
And hope to make that shift that aims for glory
Friends we were and friends we should part
You will always live tall in my heart

    Despite all the pain and misery, we still loved him, getting him to quit was impossible. As he always said to us this is how he wanted to live and die. Mr. Hyde was pure destruction, sadistic in nature, controlling to unbearable ends repetitive like a broken tape recorder he would keep repeating things over and over. Felt like he was breathing down our necks all the time. My father would come and go over the years but would eventually completely disappear. Is this how the universe had planned out his life. Or did he really have a choice to turn his life around, the most difficult part was not being abused by him, the difficult part was being helpless and not being able to help him and love him. The difficult part was watching him destroy himself right before our eyes despite all the help and support we tried to get him. There are many painful things one can experience in one's life. One among them is watching a great individual fall to addiction. There is not a more painful experience trying to help this person recover and come out of his affliction. I believe Addicts are people who try to escape emotions that are way too painful for them to process, and they medicate on their poison of choosing to get the relief and escape from their problems. Towards the end of my father's life, it was hard to be close to him. He drank himself to death, guess he knew he was becoming a burden to us and so he was taking desperate measures to end his life. For him, in his mind there was no other way out. Like all great love stories, he died in a sober mood being regretful on how he treated my mother, asked forgiveness enquired about his children. Told her what he wished the best for them in their future and silently just like that sitting on his bed passed. To tell you the truth, though he put us through a great ordeal of pain and suffering, he was doing to us, what he felt within himself. We all felt his pain and misery, his helplessness, his fear, and his desperate cries to be heard. We failed him, by trying to save our own asses and that was a terrible thing I know in my heart I will not be forgiven for that. He was an incredible loving sensitive thoughtful person, in his heart he was pure with fond emotions of friendship, love and the desire to help people. He always charged his patients a minimal consultation fee, he fought against hospital policies that put profits first than human lives. He always thought about the little guy and always appreciated the small things in life. He always told me nothing matters in this world but the small things in life. Hold on to them he told, the small things will only and always be the reason for your happiness. I know my words don't do any justice to this great man who I had the privilege to call my father. A life without him has left a very painful space in me. I just wish things were different but in this version of life's story I guess this is how it was meant to be.

The reason I said I witnessed the greatest love story is because my mother never gave up on my father ever. Despite all the abuse she devoted her life to him. Any sane woman would have left, but she stayed, and she fought for him and on top of that she did her best in all her power to make a home. It wasn't easy to any extend for her, I would say she was mad to have stayed, no matter the amount of pain she had to go through she woke up every morning and loved her husband the best that she could. Us kids have told her several times to leave him, but it only went to deaf ears. Sometimes he would make it impossible for her to live in that house and she would go away take a break but always come back to him. Because she knew nobody else would have cared for him if she left. True love stories aren't about sunsets, roses, and love letters along with the other sugar-coated stuff, they are just a small part of love, real love begins when you decide to put away your comfort and you make a sacrifice so big that cost you your time, dignity, safety, life, and respect, without requiring anything in return. She always told me, she knows the man she married, the real man behind the addiction loved her, cared for her, and did wonderful things for her before he turned into an addict. "Maybe you will abandon your love, but I will not," this is what she told me. If it was any other woman in her place my father would have died way long before the day, he died. She was the reason he survived for that long, she was his life.

# Chapter 4
# I Want to Know What Love Is

Foreigner was signing, "I want to know what love is." It was broken heart season. My roommate's long-time girlfriend dumped him, and she was on her way to marry someone else, and he was on the floor drinking. Venessa was marrying the Kite, I wasn't particularly sad about it and the same time wasn't thrilled either, my only concern was I have completely run out of the shrooms, and the weed will run out soon. The Kite was being a total ass since his meeting with Venessa he has cleaned up and quit smoking and now settled down with his future wife, he had given up on his drug days and now lives a completely sober life. My roommate poured me a drink and while Foreigner went on asking for his need-to-know what love is and asking for someone to show him. My roommate was deep in his agony of having lost his long-time girlfriend. He was really torn, and he sang along with Foreigner on the floor replaying each event of his past wondering how his relationship ended with his now ex-girlfriend.

Love, what is love? Why is it of such high value in human lives. Why hasn't any business tycoon figured out to sell love so all the heart broken ones could bounce back without having to go through a great deal of pain for a period in their lives. I believe it would be a very successful business venture and I would also estimate even without taking a statistic survey that there are more broken-hearted people than completely happy and satisfied ones. Some don't even recover; some end up killing themselves. For me when I got my heart broken, it made me question everything in myself. I had to re-invent myself top to bottom. In order to achieve that I had to completely break free and take this path of destruction, I call it "Art of self-destruction." The pain made me look at myself in a way I haven't before, and I felt sorry for myself. I knew I had to transform but the process was briefly interrupted by my love for alcohol and other stuff. My roommate would burst into tears, sing along with the song, and pour himself a drink. His story is hilarious, his girlfriend of ten years since his late teens broke it off with him and is now engaged to his neighbor's son back in his home country, imagine the odds of that happening. They broke up on a dinner date he planned to propose, he proposed and when he asked her to marry her, he said the wrong name. So instead of saying please can you marry me apple he said please can you marry my pineapple. It was close but completely a different fruit.

He had no clue why he said that and how such a blunder could happen. So, apple wanted to know why he said pineapple's name, and honestly, he did not have anything going on with pineapple. She broke it off then and there, this was like eight months ago and today she has updated her Facebook status as in a relationship with neighbor's son. My roommate felt like she must have deliberately gotten engaged to his neighbor's son so she can torment him for the rest of his life. For the last eight months he has been trying to win her back, and she, skillfully played him well, and not until today she disclosed to him, that she was engaged. She just couldn't forgive him as she always suspected he liked pineapple who was a cousin of hers. She always felt he was unusually friendly with her whenever she dropped by. But the truth was my roommate was a gem of a guy and what she thought wasn't the truth at all. He tried convincing her for the last eight months. Love is such a strange thing, battles have been fought for love, monuments have been built for love, stories have been written on love and movies have been made on love. For love, a man will literally do anything.

My roommate, from now on will be referred to as roomie, was a gentle kind loving man. He believed that he was so lucky to having found apple his ex-girlfriend because he thinks he will never find another girl to love him again. He was kind of a book worm, a geek who found nothing interesting than his books. Until apple came along, Apple loved his gentle soul and found his intelligence very attractive. It was Apple who pursued roomie, roomie was very taken aback and found her odd at first. He thought it was a joke, and she was pranking him. But eventually, after seeing her persistence and finding her feeling genuine he gave in and hence began his doom. Once a woman finds her way into a man's heart, then she owns the man. Yes, owns the man, like a handbag, and that is what I felt he was to her a handbag. He clung onto her knowing he got mighty lucky in his life and always followed her lead. But what do I know about love? I was numb in my heart feeling no emotion. A walking zombie so I shouldn't be the one to judge.

Roomie was passing through the threshold of drunk-to-shit face. He wouldn't shut up about Apple and his love story and he kept telling it in a loop while he was in the drunk phase. Now that he reached the shit faced stage, he was cursing her and accusing her of being a completely heartless woman. After the accusations he would then cry and say she was the best, she was the one, he would keep repeating Oh God, I love her, I love her. Now this was going on for a while, I started growing tired of hearing his sob story. I had to do something as he kept drinking, I had to stop him before he reached the "I want to see her now" phase. And just when I thought that he said, "I want to see her now." I told him it was a very bad idea, but he kept insisting. He began to walk towards the door to go see her. But I somehow consoled him and asked him to relax. I told him I would take him to her but after a couple of more drinks. He was calm and felt emotionally supported now that I offered to help. He would go on for the next 30 mins telling me how great I am, and I was the best roommate he ever had.

    I was hoping he would pass out but no, my man was up and still ready to go see his ex. So, I had no other option but to get him to the "Fuck it" phase. A couple of more drinks after we set off, on the way I kept telling him that he's making a big mistake and a guy like him could get any girl in the world. I consoled him more and told him I understand his pain, but a real man should hold his head high and move on once he gets dumped. I told him to quit being a baby and take life as it is, I told him to man up face his pain and quit being apple's handbag. I told him about the club we were heading to, and gave him a bigger than life kind of pitch about the place. I went on giving him a big speech on self-worth and blah that and blah this. And I was waiting for him to react and say those golden words and finally, he looked at me and said, "Fuck it, let's do it." And just like that we went to this club, drank more, and danced a lot, Roomie was all over the placed talking and mingling. The night ended well and just like that he moved on.

It's that only emotion that gives you a sense that you are truly alive, love sets you free. And everyone is learning about love. I really doubt there is anybody who has figured it out entirely, love and pain are deeply connected. The more pain you can process and overcome and be at peace, the more love you can truly feel. I wonder why we have emotions at all, being controlled by them could be a nightmare. Trust me I would know; I love myself but all those times I had to drink than live a healthy life I couldn't stop myself. There were so many emotions all tangled inside me I couldn't even recognize which ones are which and reacting on autopilot seemed like the only way forward. The pain to process was too much I had so many emotions that I repressed, put away and not processed in the right way, for all these years and suddenly now they are all coming up and out to get me. Making me behave in ways I know its damaging, but I couldn't stop myself. Felt like I was holding a loaded gun to my head and repeatedly firing it.

I wondered if I really understood what it meant to love myself, since I'm on a self-sabotaging spree day after day, month after month, maybe I really forgot what it was like to love, or I am lying to myself and in denial. But I never honestly knew what was happening to me, I was on autopilot out of control calmly witnessing my destruction. I panicked a lot in the beginning but later I just gave in and surrendered to the chaos. The easy way was not resisting it because it brought more pain, and I couldn't handle it. Letting it happen and just observing it calmly felt like the only way. It wasn't easy one bit, I brought about many situations that brought more grief, situations where I felt only defeat, sadness, anger. And in cycles I went through it one by one, hoping that someday I would wake up and be free, free to control my own life, free to breath and do whatever I like in a creative constructive way. But this storm I had to face, and storm was exactly how I felt inside me never seemed to end. Love was something too difficult to understand at this part of my life as without getting to feel it how can you begin to understand it. My life was all the grey and dark parts apart from the emotions of love. Years I've lived falling, deeper inside myself hoping to fix the parts that were broken so I can live again. The addictions the long stints of bad luck and hardships that came along in my life had a story to tell me and I had lessons to learn.

I completely agree with Foreigner I don't know what love is and I hoped someone would show me. I had several spots in the city where I would go just to sit and be alone. These were my secret spots where no one knew about. Some of these places would be in a middle of a crowd, some near the sea, parking lots. This was the part of my life where I could not sleep, my mind was turned on all the time, it was thinking and thinking, in order to escape from stressful situations and depending on the mood, I would escape to one of these spots. I lived my life spontaneously, without questioning my behavior because I was done resisting it, I had great big ambitions and dreams but however the only thing I felt like doing at that time was to drink and get high. I would do my job, I mean work hard, even if I didn't like it, I had to survive I needed that job. I was confused, I did not know what it is I should do with my life; I had no idea what I should do to achieve those dreams. And the work I did, no matter how much I worked, or how well I did my job I was always unappreciated, always controlled and constantly criticized. It was tiring, so I'd have a couple of drinks and escape to my favorite spots and drink more there, trying to solve this mystery we called life.

I see many people around me thrive well, but I just couldn't reach their level despite all the efforts. Life itself was discouraging me, it was a time for rejection after rejections, if I applied for a new job I'd be rejected, if I was called for the interview and after being interviewed rejected. If I met someone nice and when things would start of well, in a couple of months I'd be rejected. I just did not know what to do, I tried and tried and tried but everywhere I ventured seemed like I would end up in a dead end. I wanted to win so bad, but I failed very well. Felt so stuck like God pinned me somewhere I could not move nor make any progress, my life felt stagnated in a uselessness feeling like God had writers block and he just could not decide what next would happen in my life cause nothing I did worked for me.

How do you stay positive at these moments, you really have to pretend, I guess? In every level and every cell in my body I knew something was wrong, I felt the imbalance in me, and I couldn't figure out why the degree of crapness was dialed up to a 100 for me alone. And I was tired of taking all the bullshit despite all the work I've been putting in. Sitting in my office hungover from the previous night I felt an urge to escape, disappear for a while. I planned to go to one of my hideouts after work and reflect on my life, what I needed was a new plan. A plan that would work and set me free. I went to the office washroom and rolled myself a big fat joint to help me through the day. I went to the company's storeroom smoked it and went back to the office.

My anxiety seemed to be reducing and I reached the safe space, I was feeling wonderful and happy once gain. Foreigner was playing very softly; didn't know why I was stuck to this song.

I take my job seriously and I promise you when I tell you that I do not smoke weed in the office often, I am being very honest. Sometimes my anxiety levels are off the roof, and I smoke in these situations, I smoke a joint to calm down. I just remembered that I had a meeting in five minutes and metaphorically speaking of the high I was experiencing, the flight was taxing all this while and just taken off. I was super, super relaxed maybe a tad bit way too much for a professional meeting. I was sitting beside my boss facing the two gentlemen and a lovely lady from Z company who were supplying tiles. I was sitting there with a gleaming smile, and I couldn't stop smiling. It was like it was stuck to my face with superglue. Do you remember the flight that took off? Well it had reached 30,000 feet cruising altitude and my smile got bigger. I guess the people from Z company must have felt that I was very glad to meet them, and they kept glancing back at me from time to time and they would smile back.

In my head I would be telling myself to stop smiling, but I couldn't. the meeting went on for 25 minutes and I successfully finished my first meeting high. Finally, at the end of the day, the moment the clock struck 5:00 pm I was in my car driving to the beach. On the way I stopped bought a case of beer, lit a joint and continued driving towards the beach. It was at a reserve part of town and not many people knew about the place as it was hidden by a cluster of villas and a bridge.

Sometimes I felt I was the only person who knew about the place as whenever I was there, I was the only one.

Finally, I arrived at the beach, I parked my car and walked to my spot, opened a beer sat there sipping on the beer staring at the sun about to set. Most of the days when I planned to come to this spot, I would start off feeling I should drive there but when I got there, I'll have no idea why, and every time I would end up at the place, I would wonder why I even drove all this way here. What am I looking for, there was a constant feeling of a need to get away from the crowd, the urge to run away and disappear, this feeling kept growing and I never knew why I felt so? What was I running away from, I couldn't figure out anything, so many emotions in me jumbled up I couldn't identify which one is which and what all these feeling meant and what I was supposed to do with it? Was far easier to drink and try to forget about the uncomfortable feelings that kept popping up. The sound of the waves was a soothing sound, sometimes I felt they were trying to tell me something. I was staring at a giant ball of orange disappearing into the horizon and as it disappeared, and darkness began to fall.

I used to have flashes and blurry memories of her, her name will never be spoken. I have no idea why she came into my life. Felt like she broke all the cosmic rules to be with me, I thought I had no choice than to accept the way the whole thing happened, it felt amazing, and everything unfolded like the heavens conspired to make it happen but at the speed she came she left. Unlike any other breakup this one changed me forever in an irrevocable irreversible way. It turned everything inside out and changed me forever she left taking a part of me forever with her. The pain that I felt was unlike anything I experienced. I felt a constant numbness in my heart that went right up to the tip of my tongue, and I couldn't explain what that was. I felt like the spiritual heart that sits deep in my chest was bruised and it bleed invisible blood. It was the start of my derailment, I wasn't the scorn lover and trust me I did not miss her one bit, I just felt pain all the time.

I opened the next can of beer and lit the next joint, how did this happen to me, the heavens tricked me or did I trick myself into it. What is this pain I'm still experiencing, and it's been a couple of years now and I still can't figure out how I can get rid of this pain I'm experiencing? In this pain a new man was being forged. It is true the saying, "Destruction happens making a lot of noise, and creation happens quietly." My destruction was loud, the drinking increased day after day and the joints were rolled at a faster rate. I got so good I could roll a joint in the dark with one hand. But while I was destroying myself quietly in a very strange way, I was also re-creating myself, but I never ever noticed that at that time. I was always distracted by the noise my destruction made.

The connection I had with her was out of this world, she always felt like a part of me, and it felt so right. I cannot explain the way she made me feel. The connection was deep, and it was made of a strong magnetic energy that connected us in a different plane altogether.

I could feel her in me, in every way and I could feel all her emotions, and when she chose to leave, I felt that part of me was torn away when she left. I felt pain exactly how you would feel if you had your heart ripped out of your chest. The energy she left me behind with was confusion, broken confidence, panic, anxiety and a sense of loss and abandonment, pain, pain, and pain, hate, anger, and a self-esteem that seemed to have disappeared. Despite all this I honestly still hold fond feelings for her, I do not want her back and wish her the best wherever she is and hope the best for her. Now I just wanted to get out of the way I was feeling so I can move ahead with my life. But I just didn't know how to handle these emotions, these were powerful and overwhelming, and I could not direct all these energies in a positive manner, and it felt like a hell a lot of work. Healing happened very slow, and it truly felt like the old self was dying, I could not go back and be the guy I was, and I was becoming someone, new, who I still could not understand nor figure out as he wasn't formed yet.

 The new me forming had a very powerful presence in me and I felt anxious all the time as I started to do things that wasn't like the old me. I even googled and researched about people being possessed by demons, I had doubts if I was possessed. I was completely a night person, that was when I came alive, the need for constant adventure, a new thrill-seeking behavior woke up in me. All it wanted to do was have a real fun time doing everything and anything it wanted without any restriction and without any rules. It wanted to be free and feel good and escape all this pain, I was very excited and petrified to be this person. Cause in one way I was having fun in a very reckless and irresponsible way which I never had or got to do while growing up. Same time it made me feel very anxious and sacred cause I couldn't control it and feared I would turn up like my father. I woke up every morning shivering and anxious wondering what was happening to me, I enjoyed the thrill seeking at the same time I was worried that, what I was doing wasn't constructive and would not lead me to my goals and dreams. Slowly in time the real me began to disappear, it was a long and hard-fought death. My old self was really scared and worried about what would happen next in my life and if he completely let do and reluctantly accepted this death, what would become of me was his fear. I would turn out exactly like my father which is exactly the opposite of what I wanted, and I just couldn't put my mother through it all again.

But I couldn't keep resisting this horrific change that took place in me, I just didn't have any strength to resist it as it got more and more painful. And each day would be a day I would let things go a little and give in to this dark side. It demanded by attention; it just took over me not quietly but in a loud scary way. During the day I was sober, I was anxious, agitated, angry and hated being around people. All I could think of was running away to get my medicine so I could feel calm again and feel some form of joy and happiness. And every time I escaped to the beach and each instance, I witnessed the sun set and the darkness takeover I felt the sun set inside of me and my darkness took over my life a little more each trip. The helplessness and feeling of being trapped in this vicious cycle of stopping this darkness was tiring and the resistance I was putting up against myself was all too much for me to handle. I just wanted to give in, I just wanted to rest for a while without fearing my own self. I wanted to trust the darkness in me maybe he's got something to tell me and I'm refusing to listen.

I was moving to a place completely devoid of love, it was a twisted, dark place that presented itself in the form of fun and relief but secretly had consequences that were hard to escape from. When you refuse to take a long hard look at yourself and notice how you're losing the way there is no saving you I promise you that. You can wake up later at a stage where more work will have to be done to save yourself but the more you stick around dabbling in the dark side the more dangerous and difficult it gets for you to come out of it. But I was deep in the emotion of it, I was mesmerized by its power over me, it felt wrong to give in to it but also it felt like I had no other choice and was a relief in a way as I couldn't resist it anymore.

Suddenly, it felt like the Devil was given special permission to wreak havoc on me. If you'd ask me in ten years' time if I'd regretted giving in to the dark side, I'd say no, no I seriously did not regret it, to be honest I enjoyed it but no matter how wild and amazing the ride was deep down inside I wanted other things as well so even the darkness had some sort of a resistance. My wild side was fun beyond imagination all my creative force was used to get all kinds of thrills. Bar hopping most nights drinking like a fiend quenching my thirst, the first thing I would do when I woke up would be smoke a joint and eat some shrooms along with my breakfast. Work would be so much fun cause I was high, and I'd do a great job and my boss was so impressed by my work he recommended for a raise not once, not twice but three times. Even though life seemed to be looking up on the outside on the inside even after all the fun and thrills it gave me, one-night stands and raise at work couldn't keep me satisfied and happy. So, the abuse of all the drugs and alcohol got worse, I needed to keep increasing my doses each day in order to have the same level or better the previous trip I had the previous day.

I had stars and unicorns shooting out of my laptop screen. *And I worked harder everyday thinking this would be the way*

*I'd turn my life around,* I thought. My behavior kept reminding me of my father, but whatever I was doing felt like I was doing the right thing, I felt like this was my path, and resisting it felt painful as hell. I wondered if this was how my father felt during his time? I wondered if what was happening in my life was a way by the universe to show me how he felt, so I could understand him. As I know for a fact nobody understood him as much as I did. And if I was going through what he went through, I completely understand him now. The constant state of confusion of deciding what to do with life and being frustrated and angry with life for not turning out the way he planned, and the helplessness, and the need to medicate to feel some peace. The pain that seemed to control everything and that kept him hooked on the drinks. I understood all his struggles better than anyone else ever could.

I wondered why my life too is turning out the same way? Is this some sort of a family curse? Me of all the people who spend majority of my life busting my ass of so I'd get somewhere in life ended up exactly where I promised myself that I will not. I had no answers to my questions, and I felt sacred for myself, there where so many voices in my head and I couldn't think nor feel my true self, somehow it felt like I was feeling other people's pain which were not mine as I couldn't feel my own self anywhere in me. I was lost, lost not like in a regular lost way, I was really gone to an extend I had no clue what I was doing, I was scared and petrified of what I was becoming and couldn't stop myself as it didn't feel like I was in control, I had no clue how to fix this situation and even when I attempted at achieving my goals it felt fucking impossible as I would get rejected and rejected and rejected. I would have personally applied to at least 4000 jobs in a span of three years, and I was rejected for all of them. The only thing that worked for me was the drinking and the drugs and the loose women. But even that didn't feel good, though it made me feel good for a couple of hours but every time I woke up sober, I would feel like I lost a little part of me and felt like I should stop what I was doing and change my ways and deal with the pain. But it never got to that, not for now, not definitely at this part of the story. At this part of the story, I was meant to drown.

During this time, I never slept so at least I didn't have nightmares but in my real life I was living them. Constantly broke living from paycheck to paycheck, drowning in one's own sorrow. I guess it's time to head back to my car and head home. On the way home when I turned on the radio, Foreigner was on, and the song that played was *I want to know what love is*. I guess there would have not been no greater coincidence for this song to come on. Reminding me that somewhere deep in my heart I agreed with the song and was looking to fall in love with myself once again.

# Chapter 5
# The Shaman

There was a rumor going around about a shaman that lived deep in the forest with the tribal people. They were called the Akai tribe and they were a very peaceful tribe that lived in forest. The tribal people were educated as the Government had setup a school for their children. Despite the many facilities offered to them they forbid certain offers like roads as they did not want to be found and accepted into modern society some facilities like schools and a small hospital were set up for them which they agreed, but they choose to live reclusively deep in the forest to preserve their community. Over the years many tribesmen did move around some worked in the city some in smaller towns surrounding the city though the majority still lived deep in the forest. There were stories of a powerful Shaman who had travelled far and wide and on his return to his people he would educate them of the travels he has been on and things he has seen. This was a man said to be easily into his late nineties but was healthy as an Ox. There were rumors of his return which very few people knew about, the Akai were very reserve when it came to matters of their community, they have held on to secrets of the lands around them for centuries. And the return of the

Shaman was an auspicious day for them all as this was the longest period he had stayed away; it has been 15 years since he left them the last time, and many believed him to be dead.

I knew a member of the Akai, his name was Rahu, Rahu was my dealer, I bought shrooms and weed from him and sometimes other stuff when I grew tired of the shrooms and weed. Rahu used to tell me stories of his tribe, how it was growing up in the forest and he was the one who told me about the shaman and a mysterious potion he prepares that makes one sees hallucinations like no other drug. This was a ritual that was mainly done to young members of the tribe when they came to age to initiate them into the tribe, some sort of baptism or ritual followed for generations, the potion reveals inner demons that lay deep within the sub-conscious which they were meant to conquer. He said that he used to be this Shamans help and in the spare time he used to share this mysterious drug with Rahu. Rahu told me he saw things and beings he cannot describe, everything felt so real that when he woke up from his trip, he was very calm and happy. I was very intrigued and pestered him to get me some but always he replied saying he doesn't know to make the potion and only the shamans knew the secret to making it.

Like any normal Friday I was on the way to Rahu to score my usual, guess I arrived at the correct time because he was packed ready to leave. He immediately handed the stuff to me and told me he will collect the money later. Normally we smoke a couple of joints and then I split but I felt something was wrong, because he seemed to be in a hurry. I enquired if everything was alright with him and Rahu replied, "Yes but I'm in a hurry to catch the bus."

"You're leaving?"

"Yes," he replied.

"Will you come back?"

"Yes," he replied.

"Is everything okay, Rahu?"

"Yes," he replied again. At this point I knew something was up, so I kept pestering him and finally he blurted out that his master the shaman is back. I begged him to take me with him, I offered to drive him and finally he agreed after a lot of convincing.

He rolled up a joint and lit it and started to smoke it, we were on our way to Rahu's village which was a five-hour journey by road and then one-point onwards-five hour's walk into the forest. He began telling me stories of the Shaman how he travelled all over the world to collect knowledge about mysticism, my whole trip to the village was captivated by stories of the shaman and I was hooked. I just couldn't wait to get there as I had many questions to ask him. I wanted to experience that mystery drug he had, I wanted to ask his help to heal me. He could be the answer to a lot of my problems. I wasn't the superstitious kind but at this moment in my life I would pretty much ask anyone for help. Five hours later, we reached the spot where we had to leave by foot. Rahu asked me to wait in the car and not come out until he comes back to get me.

I was a bit suspicious if he'll abandon me, but it was just my doubts as the people of the forest never betray. They seem like hostile people, but the truth about them is their hostility was mainly to protect their community from outside people but once they accepted you, you become family to them. Finally, just before sunset Rahu arrives with several other people. He gestures me to get out of the car and I get out, each person embraces me and welcomes me. An old man offers me something strange to eat, trust me I have no clue what it was, and Rahu said I must eat it as it would offend him if I refused and so I ate it and all of us headed back to the village. The skies were lit in orange light the sun would soon be down and as dusk settled in everything went pitch black, I began to feel strange. I felt like I wasn't walking but floating, I kid you not I looked down on the ground and it felt like I was levitating a few inches above the ground, and I was floating and magically moving with the Akai who have come to greet me. My body temperature was rising and then it would cool down and I began to feel a bit sick. All the leaves were touching me, they gently tapped me on my shoulders in a friendly way. My body temperature would go up to a point I would feel so hot that I would think I was about to explode because of the heat and then an explosive cool wave would sweep through my body, and my body would immediately start cooling. I wanted to ask Rahu what it was that I ate, but I had no energy to talk as I had to keep up with the Akai who were moving at an incredible pace. I heard voices, gentle soft child-like voices, I wasn't sure what they were saying, and the voices grew in number as my eyes began adjusting to the darkness. The leaves and branches continued to tap me gently on my shoulder. Felt like I was about to black out, my eye lids were getting heavy, they were slowly closing in on me. I called out to Rahu, and he turned, and I could see him and his friends all looking at me, my eyes closed and opened, a sudden ringing began in my ears and then felt like someone knocked me out cold.

The next thing I knew was waking up in a hut, I was still feeling a bit drowsy, I could hear chanting coming from outside and light from a big fire bending past the drapes. I got up and walked outside, and everyone turned, it felt like they were all waiting for me the sea of people parted and made a path for me leading to the big bonfire. I was having tunnel vision I couldn't see anything clearly; everything was a blur, and the people were guiding me to the bon fire. My vision was getting better as I neared the fire, I was a bit dazed I couldn't understand what was happening and at distance I could see blurry images of two people standing next to the fire. The chanting grew louder and louder as I neared them.

When I got closer to the fire, I noticed it was Rahu and I felt a relief having seen a familiar face and he said to relax and let whatever happens to happen without any resistance. He held my hand and led me around the fire and there he was the Shaman. His body was covered with a red powder and his face with a yellow-colored powder. Around his eyes he had white, long white beard and hair. He looked calm and he gazed at me, it felt like he saw through my whole being. Rahu set me beside the Shaman who was stirring a pot, few other people joined the circle around the fire. The chanting stopped and it was silent, I could feel that it had rained as the leaves were still dripping water, and droplets of water on the trees seemed to glow in a florescent green color. Strange thing was everything seemed to glow, and the colors looked thick like paint. A drop of water fell on my shoulder from a tree above and I could see the thick fluorescent droplet flow down my shoulder. I was gestured to sit by the shaman and everyone else sat along with me. I felt the warm air from the fire warm the parts of the body facing it and the cool breeze from the trees behind me cool my back. The shaman stopped stirring and poured a strange looking substance in a big bowl and passed it, each one took a sip and it finally reached me. The shaman gestured me to drink up the balance of it, it tasted awful, and it had a very pungent smell, I gulped it all down in one go and set the bowl on the floor. Everyone began to hum in a very deep tone, I felt like I was getting drunk, and my head was spinning, something about the fire caught my attention. Two birds flew out of the fire and the birds were fire itself in the shape of birds. These two birds flew very close to me; it hovered a few feet or so from my face. Now it had my complete attention, and it started to fly around the fire. Then more birds I'm calling them fire birds emerged and they all were flying around the fire.

The shaman called out my name, I looked at him surprised wondering how he knew my name. As I turned and looked at him, he grabbed my head gently with one hand and with the other pressed a finger on my forehead between my eyes. At that instant I felt like I was thrown out of my body. I couldn't clearly see anything around me but colors, I was being pulled from behind and I wasn't sure if I was on the ground or in the air. Air was flowing past me, and I was being pulled at a great speed, the colors around me mixed and were flowing and forming a tunnel around me. I had no clue what was happening, *I must be tripping*, I thought to myself. And then suddenly, the whole thing ended abruptly, and I felt like I was thrown forward to the ground. Every cell in my body hurt and it took a couple of minutes for me to regain my consciousness.

When I woke up, I was in a completely different place, and I had no clue where I was. To make things weird it was day, and the sun was shining bright in the sky. I was lying in an open grass land, I was a bit worried, and I began to panic, as I did not know what was happening. It couldn't have been a trip because it felt so real, and my body ached from the fall and I could smell the grass, feel the warmth of the sun on my skin. The strangeness even grew when I noticed I could see other planets in the sky. There was no one around and it was so quiet, what am I supposed to do here I wondered. As I got up to my feet, I saw a lake at the end of the grassland and mountains beyond the lake. Something told me I must walk up to the mountain. Intuitively I felt that someone important was waiting for me on the mountain. I started walking towards the lake that's when I noticed behind me on the opposite direction of the lake the grasslands ended into a black foamy void, there was dark black clouds in the sky over that part of the land. And I could see several eyes, bright white eyes looking at me. That whole place didn't seem too friendly. And the next instinct I felt was to hurry and get to the mountains as soon as possible. The grass lands seemed to stretch for acres and acres, and I wondered if this was a trip it was a bad one, but not even for a second did it feel like I was tripping, everything that I was experiencing was so real, I haven't experienced anything like this before. I would glance back every now and then and it felt like the darkness was catching up to me. It looked like thick black fog, and it was making its way around the grass land, I was worried if I would be trapped in it. And the white blazing eyes kept moving along the borders of the thick black fog as it advanced, something in that fog was out to get me and there were several of them.

From the distance where I stood the black fog seemed to appear like a giant man in the form of a thick smoky fog with its arms emerging from within moving around the grass land. Maybe it was trying to prevent me from getting to the lake as the arms that extended out of the fog and was moving at a considerable pace around the grassland to trap me. At that instant I was running as fast as I could to get to the lake. But no matter how fast I ran it felt I was running at the same spot because the black fog was approaching faster, and the arms were extending faster and the gap for me to escape into the lake was becoming shorter and shorter. I was tired and I couldn't run anymore, I fell on the grass praying to God to save me, I knew I wasn't going to make it. Lying on the grass I glanced at the black fog to check its progress and was surprised to see that it has stopped, I sat up looking at it and was confused about what was going on. *It has stopped moving, what the hell is happening,* I thought to myself, *I wondered what would happen if I walked towards it.* I knew it was a bad idea but anyway I thought I'd give it a try. So theoretically, the closer I move towards the fog it should move away from me. So, I started walking towards it and as expected the black fog did move back. And that's when I saw it, wolves, the white eyes belonged to wolves, with blazing white eyes and their canine teeth and claws glows lightening white they aggressively growled and leaped, they were big, as big as Rhinos and their bodies were made of the black fog. They leapt out of the fog trying to escape it, but the light prevented them to come any further.

They were spread out all over the edge. I stood there and watched them trying to leap out of the fog, but they would get dragged back into the fog, they could move only within the thick black fog as they were made from the fog. A chill ran down my spine, I kept telling myself I want to wake, I want to wake up but there was no use. Until now the sun hasn't moved from its spot, but it looked like the planets I saw in the sky were moving. Until now I thought there would be no night as the sun didn't move but I haven't paid attention to the planets. The planets were moving, and I had to get to the lake as soon as possible before one of the planets cover up the sun. I had no choice and so I dashed in the direction of the lake as fast as I could. The black fog presumed its pursuit to catch me, dramatic music playing the whole thing seemed like I was trapped in a movie, my hair bounced in the air in slow motion, I guess there was a change in the atmospheric properties on the planet I was in, it was being effected by the other planet in space coming in between us and the sun, suddenly I felt heavy, and it became harder to run. Felt like I was moving through a highly viscous fluid. Maybe it was the gravitational effects of the planet getting close to us.

This was horrible I could see the black fog move in as it didn't seem to be affected by the changes I was experiencing. Oh God, I thought I would be eaten alive by these wolves in slow motion, I would feel each instant of the bite while it torn through my flesh. Felt like there was no hope for me but death. Wish I would wake up now, it was beginning to get dark the planet was approaching to block the sun. Seemed like it was going to collide into us I began to count down to my death as it was certain. And then it was darkness, I couldn't see a damn thing, but I could hear the wolves they were getting close. I knew I had some time before they could reach me. My first instinct was to hide but where in the grass, it would be totally useless as the whole place was flat and open. I decided to keep running and fight them when it was time. I was wondering why it was taking time for the planet to move out of the way of the sun. It was raining heavily with strong winds I could see the wolves approaching, their teeth shinning white light and claws like lightening their bodies made of thick fog, their bodies began to form as they approached me. I was on my knees looking up as I watched them approach me, there were 12 of them. They surrounded me and the leader of the pack slowly made his way through from back of the pack, he walked right up to me, and his face was hardly a foot from mine. He smelled like coal, his bright white eyes and white teeth glowing in the dark, he was growling and snarling while he circled me. I did not know what to do, I was very scared and out of ideas so I surrendered and hoped the wolves would finish me quickly, I did not want to suffer. But luck was on my side, the planet moved out and a ray of light pierced through the thick black fog and made its way right between me and the Alpha wolf. Slowly but consistently more rays of light came from the skies and lit up the grass lands once again. It was a relief lying on the grass and seeing the blue sky above me. When I got back on my feet, the fog was gone it was nowhere to be found.

*The lake seemed to have moved closer to me, maybe these are tests,* I thoughts to myself, *felt like I was put here to face my demons.* The lake was so beautiful words cannot explain its beauty, it was vast, like an ocean. The lake perfectly reflected the blue sky and the mountain, and the water was so clear, I was in paradise. I was tired and wanted to sleep, so I lay close to the shore and fell asleep. I was dreaming about my parents, I was back home, and the house was a wonderful place, I was falling asleep on my mother's lap as my father was joking and my sister laughing, we were a family once again.

I was awoken by a distant call, someone on the mountain was calling out to me. I got up and walked to the lake to wash my face. As I approached the water all I could remember seeing was a giant mouth full of teeth come at me, it was a Mosasaurus. Everything happened so fast I just remember touching the water and then a huge mouth gaped open with four-inch-long teeth come at me and then everything went dark again. I haven't quiet regained my consciousness, but I could feel that I was falling, and streams and streams of air was flowing past me, and I was falling, falling deep, deep into space. I was bewildered having no clue how I got here, I was in space falling deep into an endless void lit up by symphony of colors, I was falling through a violet cloud, then a yellow, a red cloud. The sight was breath taking, from a distance I could see something was coming towards me, I couldn't really make out, but it looked like a giant butterfly. It was communicating with me telepathically asking me not to panic and that it has come to help, as it got closer, I could see it clearer as it approached me and it was a woman, she wasn't an earthly woman, but her features were like that of an Earthly woman. I could say she wasn't from our planet because of the energy I felt from her, and her beauty was of another kind, she was angelic. Her body was covered by a white robe wrapped around her and yes, she had giant beautiful butterfly wings. Long hair that was transparent and took the color of the space behind her, she had blazing violet eyes her skin was pale white with red marking which looked like tattoos all over her body. She was at least eight feet slender, tall and a beauty that were of divine like kind.

She took my hand, and she flew me away from the colorful clouds to a white shiny planet. No, it was not cold but to my surprise was warm. I told her that I don't know how I got here and talked about the wolves and reaching the lake. She never spoke with words but with her mind. She told me that I am in the belly of the water beast. That's when I remembered the big mouth that charged at me. I asked her if I was dead or if I was dreaming all this, she giggled, smiled, and slapped me gently across the face. No, I wasn't dreaming, all this was real, I was in the belly of the water beast. She said not to panic and follow her, she led the way and we arrived at a magical door, she tapped on the door and a peep hole appeared a pair of green eyes gazed upon us and then the door which was sitting at the base of a small hill opened and we walked in. She told me her name is Violet and she is the soul of the cosmos, she introduced me to her friends Green the one who opened the door and then there was Red. Green and Red were her protectors. I asked her what she was doing in the belly of the water beast. She told me that I am being tested, my first test was the wolves, she told me that the wolves had a significant representation in my life which I must figure out for myself. She smiled lay her hand on my face and gently stroked it, I am amazed how you choose to surrender to the wolves, did you know they are mimics. I replied no, I don't understand, Violet smiled again and said if I decided to attack the wolves, they would have attacked me, they were made to do exactly what I would do and hence since I surrendered, they surrendered to me too.

Violet said there is a lesson here you must learn unfortunately she will not be able to tell me as it was my first test, the belly of the beast is your second test, the belly of the beast takes you to a different place in the cosmos depending on what your test is. The belly has transported you to the heart of the cosmos, this is the home of the souls. So, what is my test I asked, she smiled, Green and red who sat beside her were also smiling. You my friend said Violet have the toughest task to accomplish, only four souls have been here since the beginning of time. And no one has ever succeeded, I was anxious now, my heart started racing, Green placed her hands on my head and calmed me down. They asked me to rest as I would need all the energy for tomorrow. I was led to a room overlooking the sky and the sky was the stars, planets, and asteroids all which I could see crystal clear, the view was breath taking made of vibrant colors I haven't seen such beauty before ever in my life.

The sky kept changing colors and I fell asleep not knowing if all this was a dream or if it was real. I was enjoying all this strangely, somewhere between enjoying the view and having heavenly feelings lying on that bed I fell asleep. Should be many hours later or maybe I slept the whole day cause when I woke up, I felt so good. But something wasn't right, it was still night and when I looked at the time only three hours passed since I went to bed. Something woke me up, I noticed the silence, it was the kind of silence that you would maintain if you were hiding from something dreadful, a bad feeling sunk into my chest, it was a familiar feeling I had but I couldn't yet place what it was. The door creaked open slowly and some sort of white odorless smoke entered the room, the smoke stuck to floor, and it seemed like I was walking on clouds. I could hear sounds coming from downstairs, I followed the sounds which did not sound friendly at all, Violet, Green and Red were nowhere to be seen. I walked down the stairs and down the hall towards the kitchen from where the sounds were coming, I peeped through the small opening of the door and to my horror, I couldn't believe what I was looking at and I fell to the ground out of shock and horror.

I couldn't believe what I was looking at, it was the giant snake that possessed my father that made him drink, that it was for him, for me the snake was the abuse I've been through and the source of all my fears. The snake now reached a monstrous size and it seemed to be slithering through the air. The moment I hit the ground I shrieked, and it caught the snake's attention. It was about three feet wide, and 100 feet it was white colored with a black coloration along its under belly. Eyes blood red, it hissed my name, in an eerie snake like voice, it spoke, *"Oh, who have we here, yummy, yummy boy."* That is what it used to call me, 'boy.' "Come out, boy, come say hello to an old friend." My heart was pounding; all the horrors of the past came back to my mind like it was yesterday. I used to be very scared of the snake, it used to bully me mentally and blame me for anything that went wrong, it used to scare me, control everything about me, it was emotionally suffocating. He would love to fight with me. And even for a second if he sensed some joy, I knew he would come in and make sure I had twice the shitty day. Intimidating me and humiliating me was its favorite past time.

He once locked me in my dog's kennel, while the dog barked ferociously at me, he has broken my spirit to pieces, he has burnt my soul to ashes, he twisted and played with my emotions, I was completely scared of the snake, he was the epitome of evil for me, and now being a grown man, I still hid under the table scared to death. It was slithering around trying to find me, while it was following my scent, I was completely in fright and flight mode I couldn't think, I couldn't breathe, I heard a crying voice, this voice was a familiar voice, I looked around trying not to get caught and got a glimpse into the sitting room, a six-year version of my sister was sitting on the floor crying while she also hid under the table hoping the snake wouldn't catch her. The snake on the other hand was moving out of the sitting room into the kitchen, then into the hallway then up the stairs into the bedroom then out the window and then back into the sitting room through the front door. It made sure some part of its body was left hanging in every room. I signaled to my sister to stop crying and told her to hang in there tight I'll come get her. I was making my way to kitchen to get a knife. As I was crawling towards the kitchen dodging the snake's body, the plan was to grab the biggest knife to defend myself.

At a distance I could see a bright light coming into the kitchen, I grabbed a knife and slightly peeped through the window to see what it was. At a distance I could see Violet stand alongside Green and red and they were signaling me to a sword that was pierced to the ground. I jumped through the window quietly and started to run towards violet and grabbed the sword. The snake hissed I smell you, maybe I'd snack on your sister first. Violet eyes unveiled the horror unfolding back in the house and I dared not to turn back, my heart was beating at speeds I have never experienced before, I was scared what the snake will do to my sister. But I could see the horror on the face of Violet, Green and Red. I reached the sword, pulled it out from the ground. Violet whispered into my ears, "Face the demons from your past."

When I turned around, I was petrified at what I was seeing, the snake now outside the house coiled around my sister was preparing to swallow her whole in one bite. I turned towards Violet and told her I won't reach in time to prevent what was about to unfold. I couldn't run that fast. She whispered in my ears, "Believe."

With little energy left in me and a giant snake that seemed to tower over me like a skyscraper, I wasn't sure how I'd bring this beast down. The snake looked at me, with its deep red eyes staring at me, its tongue tasting my sister, and it hissed, "Yummy, yummy," and opened its giant mouth to devour her whole. I screamed and shouted out at the snake, the sight was horrific to watch, my little sister just a couple of feet away from the snake's open mouth. And just then out of an inner instinct I leapt into the air towards the snake, sword held high above my head. I was flying through the air, and I was approaching it faster, I threw the sword towards the snake. As the sword kept moving in the air towards the snake and me high in the air also taking the same trajectory of the sword, my sister's head was just about to enter the snake's mouth. From the corner of its eye, it saw the sword approaching and moved away and to my shock I witnessed the giant serpent swallow my sister. I crashed into the ground beside the snake a couple of feet away from the snake. Still in disbelief of what I witness, I exploded into a murderous rage, shouting like a mad drunk, out for vengeance I leapt 30 feet into the air and struck the colossal snake right in the head and knocked it hard into the ground. The snake surprised immediately recovered from the knock but was shaken at the strength I had. And the next second it regurgitated my sister, she was covered in slime and was unconscious, I saw Violet rush towards her, and then the battle began.

The giant snake swung it tale at me, and I was tossed high into the air, I fell back near the sword which was a little out of my reach. And then it stood in a strike pose, ready to attack, I could barely stand up at this point. Summoning every ounce of strength and courage in me I stood up and faced the snake towering over me, and like lighting it struck. I was held between its jaws and its teeth sunk into my flesh. I knew what was next and dying didn't seem like a bad idea. *At least my sister is saved,* I thought. And while it was coiling around me to swallow me, the snake put its head close to me and said let me have a taste and stuck its tongue out. I grabbed its tongue and yanked it out with all my strength. I was released from its grip and with its tongue in my hand I was fell onto the floor. The snake shook its head violently side to side in pain. I had a tooth of the snake pierced through my right thigh, and the same leg was broken in serval places. I knew I was done now and so I just lay there with tears flowing slowly out of my eyes.

The snake finally recovering from the blow still screaming in pain hurled its head towards me with mouth open, not able to move this time I took the attacking bite as it clenched me tight in its jaws. I had several of its teeth now sinking deep into my flesh and then it flung me flying several feet away. I fell right above the sword. I hid the sword under my shirt, all bloodied and defeated I lay still as the snake slithered around me picked me up and coiled itself around me and swallowed me whole and as I went down its mouth, I stuck the sword hidden under my shirt into its flesh and cut through its flesh and as it gulped me down and the sword cut through its body. It was the end for the monster snake as it lay on the ground, my hand and the sword stuck out from its body, and I could feel life leave me, as I drew the last of my breath and a deep peace filled my heart and with the feeling of triumph my eyes felt heavy, and I fell asleep.

I woke up and was back on the bed, confused and disoriented I stumbled out of bed. I wasn't feeling sick, I felt great, but my body was very weak. I dragged myself out of the bedroom and down the stairs, Violet, Green and red were sitting at a table with a feast prepared for me. They smiled back at my confused face still trying to figure out if I were dreaming or if it was real. Green held me up and placed me on the chair she stroked my head and smiled, and she whispered into my ears, "Believe." Red got up and walked towards me she too placed her hand on my head and patted my back she too whispered into my ears, "Believe." They fed me well, and my energy came flowing back into my body. Their touches seemed like it touched my soul. Green and Red then held my hand and guided me to Violet who had her back facing us standing near the main entrance.

Violet looked at me and said, "How did you sleep last night?" I told her about the dream and how real it felt. I even told her she was there, I asked her if it was real or a dream. She just smiled and said, "How do you know if you are still dreaming?" She lifted me up in her arms and bid farewell she told me that she is always beside no matter where I go but I must believe in myself before anything else in the world. She promised whenever I needed guidance or help to just close my eyes and remember her and ask for help and she will give me a sign. My body began to evaporate, and a cool breeze swept me away, the next thing I remember was being in total darkness and I was being tossed around. Felt like I was inside a moving vehicle making sudden stops and swift acceleration maneuvering in all direction. And we were ascending inclined at a fast rate. There was an intermittent deafening growl that would vibrate the surface I was sitting on. And then the climb stopped and whatever I was in seemed to move in a calm fashioned way.

I covered my ears when I heard the next growl, which was the loudest and then a sudden burst of light hit my face and I was thrown into the light. I was once again flying in the air and then landed on a clear pool of water. When I came to my senses and took a glimpse of what took me for a ride, I saw the mosasaurs leap into the air and dive back into the depths of the lake splashing water into the pool. I finally made it I have crossed the lake, at a distance, on the other side of the lake I could no longer see any dark fog, everything looked beautiful from where I sat. having no clue what to expect on my path next, I swam in the pool for some time cleaning myself and relaxing. I decided I will spend the night here and then continue with the journey the next day having rested well. I lay that night looking at the skies in wonder as it was lit by a million stars with a bright white full moon. The reflection of the night sky on the lake looked like a giant marble. It was truly beautiful never have I had such a deep connection to nature before. It felt like I was one with it, it felt like I recognized its emotion and was in sync with the universe, I felt no separation from it, I felt one with it and it felt like home.

The sun came up and it lit the sky red the shades changed as it rose into the sky, and it was a warm summer day. Hummingbirds a thousand of them were flying around dipping their beaks into flowers, bunnies hopped by along with its babies eating the grass. And as the sun's light hit the mountain it lit a long path leading to its summit. I had a tedious climb before me and so I got going. The climb wasn't difficult, but it was a long way up. Everything felt good that day and I seemed in the best of spirits climbing my way up to the summit. All kinds of beautiful friendly animals came into contact like they were all here to greet me. By mid-day I was halfway up and seemed like I would be on the summit just before the sun set.

At sunset I was nearly there but I was tired, so I planned to rest and finish the climb the next day. The next day when I woke up happy to finish my journey but instead of being nearly at the top I was back in the pool. The hummingbirds flew by me, then the bunny family hopped along, this was strange and frustrating cause now I had to do the climb all over again. This time I promised myself I will not stop until I've climbed up to the summit and finish this once and for all. I set of yet again and the climb began this time by noon I was nearly there, I was very tired, but I told myself I'll keep going until I reach the summit. But every time I reached the spot where I rested initially, I would become very tired, and I had to rest. This time I did rest but I decided I would complete the climb, after two hrs. of rest making sure I didn't fall asleep I continued with my journey and finally reached the summit. When I finally reached, I was completely disappointed as there was nothing around.

No magic door, no beast, not even a clue to what should I do next. Sitting there clueless what to do I thought maybe this is it, so I sat there and waited. I tried my best not to fall asleep and right about mid night a flash of light went in all direction with the mountain as its epicenter lighting up the skies. Then the flashes happened again and this time I stood up anticipating something to happen my heart began pounding as I had no clue to what to expect. But nothing happened but beams of lights being flashed in regular intervals. Apart from having a great view the summit looked like a dead end.

The view from up top was magnificent, the mountain was sitting on a lonely island surrounded by the lake. There was something mystical about the mountain as I felt only peace in my heart. Felt like it was giving me a gift for having achieved the climb to the top of the mountain. I had no clue what to do next or where to go felt like this was it. The next day, I woke up once again at the bottom of the mountain in the pool of water. Once again, I saw the hummingbirds fly and the rabbit family hop by, but this time I paid attention to them and while watching them hop by I realized something, they were all heading at the same direction and so I decided to follow them just out of curiosity and somewhere deep inside my heart I felt like maybe this was it. Maybe it wasn't about the mountain but where the animals were heading. So, I followed all the bunnies, they seemed to stop if they got too far and waited for me to catch up. Finally, after four hours of walking the bunny ran away, and the birds flew away and ahead of me was a door made of stone that rested at the foot of the mountain. I approached the door and before I could even try to push it, the door opened. I walked into the mountain, there was a pathway that lit by itself and as I progressed inward, it finally ended on a giant stone slab. I stepped on the stone stab and the stab started levitating up, another doorway opened, and I was transported upwards, seemed like I was heading to the summit from inside the mountain.

The stone slab stopped when it reached the farthest point of the passage and I jumped to another pathway leading to another door. And like before, before I could open it, the door swung open and inside was an old man sitting by the table wearing the thickest pair of glasses. His hair was white and old as time, his white moustache covered his lips, he glanced at me and a smile crack through his face. He said in a soft welcoming voice, "Please come in my dear, I have been expecting you." And as I approached the table he sat at; I saw a huge file with my name on it. He looked at me and said, "Ah, yes, it is your file. It has all the details of your life, the past, present, and future." I asked if I was here to learn about the future. "No," he said, "you're here to understand something more." He snapped his fingers, and the book was gone and then he stood up and said, "Please follow me." He introduced himself as the accountant. He was put in charge by the creator of the universe to maintain and alert the creator if anyone was deviating from their destiny as written by him. And so, since he was the one put in charge, he was called the accountant.

He was so thrilled having me there and said it had been ages since he last met someone. We reached a secret door on the hall, and he cleared his throat and with a serious face said, "This is as far as I can come, he has been waiting for you for a long time." I asked, "Who," and the accountant just smiled, opened the door, and shut it behind me. I entered a very large room that seemed to go on forever and at the farthest distance I could see a bright white light in the form of a human walk towards me. And as the figure of light got closer to me, he had no features but only the shape of a man. When the figure got closer, I was shocked to see it was my father, he embraced me tight and took a good look at me with a smile on his face. We spoke for a very long time I discussed everything about my life to him and he listened intently. He told all the trials in my life was there for a reason and it was time for me start believing in myself. He asked me to make peace with my past and move on in my life, and he kept hugging me every now and then, finally after a while he said he had to go, and it is time. In a loving tone he said wake up Son, and pressed his index finger on my forehead, darkness filled the room and my father seemed to disappear into the darkness I felt sleepy, and he laid me down on the floor, just before he disappeared, he said that he will always be with me and he loved more than I could ever imagine, believe in yourself son he said. Before I could say anything to him my eye lids felt heavy and began to close and then it was complete darkness.

# Chapter 6
# Way Back Home

Back in the village Rahu was preparing dinner, deer meat was cooking in a mud pot the aroma filled the room and in the corner of the room I was laid on a stack of banana leaves, slowly regaining my consciousness, felt like I was drunk and I was a little disoriented, I was so hungry I could eat a whole elephant, even before I opened my mouth Rahu handed me a plate full of deer meat, rice, pulses, and vegetables, welcome back he said. How long have I been out I asked because it felt like I was gone for days, Rahu replied three hrs., but it felt like days in my head. Rahu sat next to me and said that the Shaman wanted to see me the next day. I was thrilled to hear that as I had so many questions. I told Rahu about my experience and Rahu explained that experiences could last for a one or two hours or a couple of hours depending on what the soul wants to reveal to the person. "The soul?" I asked, he asked me to relax for the night and all my questions will be answered tomorrow. I asked Rahu about his experience, and he just smiled, he told me to keep the experiences a secret and only speak with the Shaman about it.

My first experience was very much like yours they are illusions your soul projects revealing your fears so you learn to release them, once you establish a connection and understanding with your soul, the next time you experience the portion, you will have a different experience. Out of curiosity I asked, "Like what? Tell me about it." But Rahu remained silent and said, "Somethings are meant to be experienced and not explained." Rahu had a joint rolled and he lit it and passed it to me, I wasn't sure if I had to do it as I was very tired, but he insisted and then we smoked the joint together and dug into the food. I was famished and the food was so delicious I don't have words to describe it and like Rahu said somethings you need to experience it cause even words won't be enough to describe how delicious the food was. Language a funny thing right, even simple things could be read and misinterpreted and taken out of context, and humans have evolved only to the extend to express and document things in the form of language and drawings in the early ages. I wonder what all parts of history we have misinterpreted and misunderstood the content totally out of its context. Knowledge could be a good thing but if not understood correctly and applied properly as per its real understanding, it could have disastrous results. Language has its limitation when it comes to describing experiences which is out of this world. Experiences you must experience to understand, but the moment you try to describe it by mouth or even by writing it gets impossible to capture as the experience originally occurred, and then when another person reads it the possibility of how he understands is limited to his imagination which might not be the truth.

As I enjoyed my meal, I had thoughts about the various periods of our planet wherein a divine being took birth in human form to bring forth a teaching to the people from the heavens. Knowing the nature of man and how manipulative we can be to hoard all the power and control over the masses of people, how much of history was incorrectly fed to the people to misguide the generations to keep them ignorant and keep the truth to a selective few. How honest were the people who recorded historical events centuries back, was it accurate and if it were accurate did, we translate it correctly? Are we reading the right information, though today we live in the version of the most modern world, having achieved great technological advances, the people are still misguided by the media, we are just presented portions of the truth and the truth is always hidden? I've got no proof to back this up but whenever I watch the news, I always feel that the truth is way far beyond what has been told.

Technologically we have made giant leaps but us humans are still inhuman in modern times. We have just learnt to pretend and live with the flow thinking this is the way now not knowing how controlled we are. Most of us are trapped in a life just to make ends meet or survive. And the ones who made it and doing well wants to keep everything for themselves and control the masses of people so they can continue to keep getting the benefit. If the people of today are like this now and when man lived in more primitive times without the comforts, we enjoy today don't you think they might have been way more dishonest than us or did modernization ruin us humans. Rahu looked at me as I was lost between the deer curry and my thoughts, he asked me to snap out of it. "Enjoy your meal and we will go for a walk," he said.

After my meal we headed deeper into the forest I asked him where we are heading to, all he said was, "Wait and see."

What I loved most about Rahu and his people where they were very open people who were willing to share their culture and knowledge, if they didn't see you as a threat, they were very loving, honest open people. They seemed so content and happy with their lives, for them concepts like stress, bills, taxes, addictions, divorces, birth certificate, passports, identity cards, money, banks, savings, loans, credit cards, education, were all foreign and non-existent. Mother Earth was everything to them, they got food, clothing, and shelter from the earth. They lived in harmony with the Earth. They did not want to do anything else, they roamed freely wherever they wanted, they were truly free in every sense, and they shared everything within their community. Rahu looked back at me to check if I was doing okay, he asked me if I was tired. "Not yet," I replied.

"You know the shaman was talking about you."

"Really, what did he tell you?" I asked.

"He said that you're different."

"Different?"

"Yes, different."

"In what way?"

"He didn't say that; all he said was you're different."

"Do you know that the Shaman has only rarely invited people from outside the tribe, when I spoke with him to check if I could invite you for the ritual, he nodded without even thinking, guess he was expecting you?" I was intrigued by what Rahu told me, I wondered what the reason would be. We started to climb a steep slope and Rahu said, "It's on the other side."

"What is?" I enquired.

"Wait, and watch," he replied.

After a lot of effort put to climbing that slope, we got to the top, and right in front was a small pond with crystal clear water right in the middle of the jungle. I could clearly see fish swimming around, the reflection of the tress, stars, and the crescent moon on the surface of the water. Rahu turned on his torch and put it in a transparent plastic bag and threw it into the pond. The torch sank to the bottom lighting up the pond. "What are you waiting for?" Rahu said. "Go, jump in." We swam for an hour, lay on the grass staring at the sky smoking a joint. Rahu began telling me stories of the jungle while growing up. What was meant to be a weekend to get high and eat junk food turned out to be an epic adventure. Felt like I was living there for weeks. I still couldn't believe it has been just a couple of hours since I arrived.

Felt like I spend an eternity already, I couldn't stop thinking about my meeting with the shaman the next day. I wonder what he would tell me, I was very curious and could not sleep. Under the starry night sky and the beautiful pond beside me, I wondered what life really had in store for me, when I was a kid, I has so many dreams, I had promised myself of achieving so many things and yet I sit here lost looking for my path, my way back. I was feeling a bit strange since the hallucinations I had near the fire, I haven't quite become myself yet, not a hundred per cent. Rahu was fast asleep, and his snores echoed around the pond. *I was excited about the next day what more surprises will I encounter tomorrow,* I thought. I felt like the center of the universe for all the attention I was receiving since the time I arrived at the village. Everyone in the tribe was very kind and accommodating. But never have I tripped so intensely that the dream seemed so real and waking up from that experience seemed like I woke up to the dream. This was exactly what I used to feel sometimes in the real world like I don't fit in this space, I needed to escape reality by taking some form of a drug and be part of the fantasy or dream world that would be playing in my head. I always felt that most people lived their lives pretending to be someone they truly aren't, it was all an act when they interacted with the world, I didn't know if it was them pretending or me not accepting reality. I feel like we put on various masks to survive in this world, and I didn't know why we had to do that. It was confusing to me, it just didn't feel like people were authentic as they truly were and instead there is this fake persona, they put on to be accepted, what was this need to put on this act?

The next day I woke up fresh and ready to meet the shaman. Instead of walking me to the shaman I was surprised that Rahu took me back to my car. We drove deeper into the forest until we reached an old check post. Rahu asked me to wait in the car and 30 minutes later he returned with a sack filled with some herbs. We drove back to the village and then he opened the sack and showed me the herbs in the sack, and I was surprised to see that it wasn't herbs but weed. He asked me to take as much as I wanted and charged me my nominal fees. I was overjoyed to have to restocked my supplies in quantities that I have not purchased before. Rahu told me to get ready as the shaman would be ready to see me. I was following Rahu as we jetted past people. After a couple of minutes, we reached a tent that was pitched at the corner of the entire camp. Rahu nodded his head and asked me to carry on into the tent.

My heart began to tense up and beat fast, I was anxious now my thoughts were racing, *why did he ask for me*, I thought, I entered the tent and he stood at the corner with his back turned to me. He turned around with a smile on his face and asked me to take a seat. I sat down and he sat on his chair next to me, He was looking at me with a smile on his face and he asked how are you feeling. I replied telling him I felt wonderful and thanked him for having me for the ritual, he smiled back and nodded with acknowledgement. And in a gentle voice he said not to worry, and all my troubles and worries will settle down and I would be able to view everything in my life with better clarity. We sat and discussed about my life, and he just listened to me patiently, he did not talk much but kept repeating to always looks within myself and not to worry about things that are not in my control. Finally, he tapped me on my back and said one day you will turn back and look at this day as the beginning of a great life. It seemed like he was truly impressed by me and expressed genuine fondness towards me. He told me that all the secrets of the universe are in me, and I don't have to seek for it anywhere else. He tapped me on my shoulder and said we will meet again.

I left the shaman's tent feeling like someone robbed me of all my misery and feeling refreshed. I told Rahu I need to get back to town and I walked back to the car. I started the car, the engine roared and I took off, smoking a cigarette and feeling a great urge to return to my life fully charged and rejuvenated. Felt like I was on vacation for at least two months, but it has been just a day. My mind was running from thought to thought and it was trying to remember something, but thoughts just came emerging, and I navigated through it to find what I was trying to remember. It was a moment in my past, a memory shared with my father, just before I left the shaman got up and gifted me a talisman and he whispered into my ears, "It's the small things, small things matter." These were exactly the words my father told me, and I was trying to remember that moment, I was trying to concentrate and remember the memory, but my mind just couldn't remember the day but only the words.

I decided to stop for the day and spend the night in a hotel, I was just two hours away from the city and before I reached the loud noisy city life, I wanted to enjoy the quiet and calmness of the rural life out of an impulse before I joined back the busy city circus life, plus I was feeling refreshed from the experience with the shaman and wanted more time to myself to gather my thoughts so I'd be ready to join the madness that awaited me back in the world. So, I decided to spend the night at the lake view resort my favorite place to spend weekends, I checked in to my usual room, I was sitting in the balcony looking at the night sky, the only sound I could hear where the crickets. I lit a joint and puffed it wondering what is to come in my life, what am I supposed to do with my life. I knew sitting at a desk job was not what I was looking for. Something in me told me that it was time, but I didn't know what I should be doing. I still felt like I was in the company of the shaman, the effect of his presence still lingered in me. I wasn't scared or anxious about the future I was just curious about how it will all turn out. Maybe God is sitting in his balcony looking at me with a smile on his face knowing how awesomely my life is about to change. I could feel it too in me, and it was something I was looking forward too. It was pitch dark outside, but I was beginning to see through the darkness.

A slight drizzle began, and the smell of wet earth spread around. I was getting bored and planned to take a walk, I got to the lobby no one was around. I was staying in a resort located six kms from the highway. The road leading to the resort was poorly lit and since the resort hasn't seen many customers over the years, they did not bother to cut the overgrown bushes which grew into the path from the highway to the resort. It was a calm and quiet sight in the night but the calm and quiet was too silent, silent to the point it was deafening with the absence of any sounds, the place looked like what came to existence straight from a horror movie. One of the main reasons for me to stop by in this resort is because of the story of a woman who was found dead under mysterious circumstances in the resort, the resort was very famous for pulling in crowds who were eager to experience a night of haunting, apart from that I loved the place and was a frequent customer.

Another strange incident happened which resulted in two other deaths and eventually the crowd that came to experience the hauntings stopped coming out of fear and the resort became even more famous but not many people dared to come, and the owners of the property tried selling the place, but no one would buy it hearing about the stories. Many stories spread about the resort but the one that stuck with people is that it was okay to visit the resort between January to October, November and December were the months with increased supernatural activity. Eventually, the owners kept the place open with a minimum number of staff during those months and rest of the year business was not bad. I have never experienced any supernatural event during my visits, I couldn't understand what all this fuss was about. I loved the quiet and calmness the placed brought me and, I befriended the watchman of the resort whose company I deeply enjoyed.

Nobody apart from the watchman, a maid and the chef stayed over with the guests who planned to spend the night there during the months of November and December. Well, I was not there for the haunting part, it just so happens that the place is one of my favorite places for a vacation. Apart from the ghost infestation the resort was in a very beautiful valley overlooking a lake. The food was excellent, and the place was incredibly cheap. I used to visit this resort with friends all the time and we always had a great time. Except this time, I was stuck alone and this time I wasn't feeling the festivities in the air. I found out that there was only one other couple who were there in the resort who wasn't aware of the resort's history. The watchman of the resort and I were good friends, he invited me over to his cabin by the main gate for a couple of drinks hearing I arrived. I was standing by the main entrance door looking out for signs of the watchman. But seemed like he hasn't reached yet. The time was around 7:30 pm, temperature was dropping from the afternoon heat and a light layer of mist was floating through the air engulfing the ground.

The maid approached me and asked me what I'll have for dinner; I ordered my usual duck roast and bread. A couple of minutes later I heard a whistle and when I looked out, I saw the watchman raise a bottle of rum with one hand and some roasted beef with the other. I walked towards his cabin; he was delighted to see me as it has been quiet sometime since my last visit. He said times have changed and there are rumors of a new buyer that is going to take over the resort, but nothing has happened yet. He emphasized the incidents of supernatural activity, and hauntings have increased very suspiciously since then.

Now people have started having sighting of the ghost in greater numbers, though the watchman wasn't fully convinced he wanted my help to get to the bottom of this conspiracy that have seemed to have gripped the resort lately. Having nothing else to do I agreed, the drinking began, and the watchman began telling me a very disturbing story. Two months back we had a couple visiting from the city, the guy was an engineer working for a construction company and his wife a teacher. They arrived here in the afternoon, they enjoyed their meals here and their long walks to the lake and boating in the lake. They were here for the long weekend and the first day went by well without any problems. The second night both came running out their bedrooms screaming and shouting, apparently, they heard voices in the corridor of a woman talking. When they opened the door, they didn't see anything, moments later the voice started coming out of their bathroom and they could see a shadow-like figure moving inside the bathroom.

Petrified, both ran out of their rooms, they left the next morning, but the sighting did not stop there. The watchman himself saw a figure walking through the corridor on the first floor of the resort a couple of times in the last few weeks and maybe a month and half ago. Everyone stayed over the watchman's cabin at bedtime. There were rumors that the activity was maximum at the southeastern wing, strange noises and screams were heard at around 2:00 am at nights. So that night the watchman and I decided to go down to the southeastern wing to check the place out for any supernatural activity. The strange part was the watchmen felt the whole thing was a scam as these ghosts never hurt anyone and they just seemed to walk around making scary noises with the intend to scare people. Couple of drinks in, Noam the watchman began telling me stories of his experience in the army. Noam was a retired soldier from the Israeli army, who have seen a lot of action. He also served a couple of tours for UNICEF, and he had a paranormal experience on one of his tours in Africa. In one of his tours, the location cannot be disclosed, as he says his missions were highly classified and he keeps most of stories that way with censorship to certain details. He never tells for what or why he was sent to do in a certain place, he kept details of his mission a secret. He tells me only his experiences in war, of how he was cornered or had to fight a guy with his hands and had to kill with a knife stuff like that.

In one of his tours to Africa he was deployed deep into a jungle to a small village. It was a small village that had a lake and his troop were stationed there for an indefinite period. Three months into their stay, they were facing planned attacks by the local rebels, his troop was also caught in a region that was haunted by unsolved mass murders, the locals blamed them on a demon. Every full moon day a person normally children would go missing and their bodies who be recovered couple of days after their death, 6 days to be exact on the details. Every time the cause of death seemed natural and there were no signs of violence against the victim. In the beginning the Israeli troop believed it was the rebels behind the killings but when the bodies were recovered and when no signs of mutilations or trauma was detected on the victims the soldiers grew more and more confused. Every year six people would disappear starting from the first full moon to the $6^{th}$ full moon and then the killings would stop. There has been three deaths since the soldiers arrived, the captain appointed two of his best men to investigate the killings. On the fourth full moon one among the two soldiers disappeared and the other was found in the jungle in a coma. Noam was later instructed by the captain to investigate the case further.

A body was recovered in the jungle on the sixth day since the fourth full moon and it turned out to be the body of the missing soldier. Noam found no signs of attack on the body; it was like the other deaths the heart just stopped beating. Noam went through the journals of his colleagues and found out that they were trying to trace a person and accidentally stumbled on something strange living in the woods, they did not identify what it was, so it wasn't clear if it was a person or animal, the only proof they had was the strange sounds it emitted. A series of clicking vibrating noise followed by a deep humming sound that sounded like a human in pain. Noam began his investigation and suspected the mystery behind the killings were hidden deeper in the jungle. The final entry in the journal was the day before the full moon and last clue he had was his comrades were leaving that day to visit the witch doctor. Noam began enquiring on the witch with the local people and he received various versions of her story that could not be relied on, he enquired and interrogated many people but couldn't get satisfactory and reliable intel to follow up on his lead. Just when he was about to give up and look for other clues that might solve the murder and missing case, Bandile a local who organized supplies to the army camp advised him to meet the village witch doctor who lived in a hut 33 kms into the jungle away from the village near the river. Noam met with his captain and did not tell him he might be hunting for a ghost but instead told him he had a lead and wants to investigate the witch doctor. The next day he set off with Bandile to visit the witch doctor on foot. Noam was suspecting to find a trail of clues and his hunch was right. The closer they got to the witch doctor hut the air smelt foul. The number of animal corpses started to increase in number as they approached the house. Noam planned to camp at a ridge overlooking the lake and the house where the witch lived. He wanted to observe the activities of the witch before he confronted her. Instead of camping on the ground he planned his stake out on a large tree that gave him the perfect view over the hut. Bandile was growing nervous, and his fear got the best of him so Noam relieved him and asked him to go back to the camp and inform the captain that he would return in two days.

Time was around 2:00 pm, Noam settled on a large tree branch and Bandile was on his way back to the camp, 20 days left for the next full moon. Noam documented every single detail of his investigation, a total of 37 animals were found dead along the path they took, mostly deer, birds, monkeys, and rabbits. Every carcass had their hearts removed and their internal organ were completely exposed. Some sort of a ritual was performed, remnants of burnt leaves and other unidentified substances lay around the carcasses. The smell was unbearable Noam explains it smelt like death all around. The soil was dark and moist, and it seemed like the soil was soaked in blood. As the land approached the witch's hut the air got chill and dense thick tress covered the skies enclosing the land below in a partial darkness. Noam told me he knew in this gut he was about to solve the mystery behind the deaths. Bandile was running back to the camp, he was in a state of shock having witnessed the death animals. Fear had its claws sung deep into his flesh and the mind deceived his eyes for all he could see is maleficent sights around him. His breathing got intense, and he felt like no matter how much he tried to breath he was suffocating.

Images of the witch flashed now and then in his mind, the bodies of dead animals, he felt like the ground beneath his feet was spinning. He fell to the ground, thinking that something tripped him, with petrified eyes he gazed in all directions to see if he was being followed. As he sat, there on the ground he could feel a pair of eyes on him, and his instincts told him it wasn't a friendly gaze but an evil presence with an insidious plan and he felt his life was in danger. Bandile had another 23 kms ahead and he began to feel he wasn't going to make it. A cool breeze blew towards him parting the dead leaves that lay before him on the ground. Bandile sat frozen on the ground as he gazed at a dark image move behind the dense thick tress before him playing hide and seek.

Meanwhile back on top of the tree branch Noam fell asleep, he was woken by a clicking sound. He pointed his rifle in the direction of the sound looking through his scope to find the source.

Silence, dead silence, a twig snapped in the opposite direction and Noam turned immediately the other way, silence again, Noam then looked at me topping up my glass with more rum and said, "I decided to climb down to search the place as the tress were blocking this line of sight through his scope." He silently got back on the ground, like a cat he jumped and landed on the ground quietly took cover behind the trees and then looked around in all directions and he found nothing. He looked at his watch and the time was around 5:55 pm, the sun was about to set, and his eyes were just beginning to adjust to the darkness. He could sense that someone else was around and so he slowly and quietly moved around from tree to tree taking cover and scanning the place. He made sure he didn't make any sudden movement to avoid making any sound and even controlled his breathing.

Bandile was shocked at the sight he was witnessing wondered how he would get out of this situation. He went into fright and flight mode and began running like a mad man shouting and screaming for help. He stumbled again on a log and fell down a steep sloop. He stumbled down to the foot of the sloop and looked up and could not find anything. "Am I dreaming?" he wondered. *No, this cannot happen to me,* he thought to himself, with the sun setting he knew he was in trouble? He got up and began running again scared that he is being followed by a dark shadow.

He ran as fast as his legs could carry him and never looked back, nobody knows to this day where he is because he never reached the camp nor was Bandile's body recovered and eventually he was proclaimed missing. Now that the night has set in, back on the location, Noam found footprints belonging to a human, but the prints mysterious disappeared. It was like someone walked for a distance and then suddenly vanished. Noam took note of this strange discovery and added it into his log. He then climbed another tree overlooking the hut and waited until the witch arrived. Two hours later the door of the hut swung open with some force which caught Noam's attention and for the first time he had a glimpse of the witch. She was walking to the lake, she halted just before the water undressed and then walked into the water. And just before she submerged in the water she turned sharply in the direction where Noam was smiled and then submerged into the water. That gaze she gave Noah made him very nervous, felt like she knew he was there all this while. He knew then that only the witch doctor could explain the mystery killings, because she is the one doing it. That smile she gave revealed a lot of things, it was a welcoming smile for Noam to visit his death. Behind that evil smile was the monster responsible for so many deaths over the past decades.

Noam had only one thing to do, capture her, but how he wondered, he had no clue what to anticipate after that stare. A smile he will never forget for the rest of his life. She knew he was there and no matter where he went, she knew exactly where he was. How was she doing this he wondered. The witch then turned around and walked into her hut, she walked slowly and took her time, hinting, if you dare come get me. Noam was hesitant, he knew he had to confront her now and turning back would be a big mistake. Carefully and slowly, he made his way to the hut, his heart pounding fast behind his chest, anxiety building up and his breathing grew faster as he neared. Pistol in one hand and knife on the other he made his way to the hut, the smell was unbearable, foul, and disgusting. There were bones all over the place, and the land was like stepping on quicksand, soft and sludgy. Noam knew for a fact a lot of blood has been spilled on this land as it smelled like a battlefield fresh out of battle.

Noam was about ten feet from the hut, when the door swung open, the only thing he could see was a shadow on the floor from where he stood. Step by step slowly he moved forward, he did not want to get too close and at the same time he wanted to see her completely so if she tried anything suspicious his plan was to injure her with a bullet. He needed evidence backed up with facts and a confession to be 100% sure that she was the one behind the killings of both the people and animals to take any sort of action. A shaky high-pitched voice said, "Come in Mr. Soldier Man, come in." Noam sensed a presence of grave evil not just by the surrounding but also in her voice, in his heart he wanted to put a bullet between her eyes and end it, but this training kicked in and stopped him of such a folly without the evidence.

His eyes readjusted to the light falling from the hut, she was sitting on a table, with big black eyes that seemed to pierce through his soul watching him approach and a smile cracked across her face as Noam neared the door. What brings you here at these parts of the jungle she asked maintaining her evil smile. She was looking at Noam like he was a delicious snack, a treat for her to enjoy. As soon as Noam approached the door he scanned the hut with his eyes, looking for any items and clues that could lead to any of the victims. The Witch kept persisting Noam to step in, he felt like it was an invitation to his death and then from the corner of his eye he saw a military water bottle lying in the corner of the room. Noah asked her firmly how she came into possession of the water bottle. She replied saying she found it lying on the forest. Noam proceeded to make many more enquiries, but she became silent; he could sense the frustration built in her. Noam told her that she is under arrest, and he will have to take her into his custody for further questioning. "Where to?" she asked. Noam replied, "To the military camp," and in a fraction of a second, she leapt forward.

Noam pulled the trigger and the bullet hit her on her leg, she screamed in pain and tried to leap on him again and this time the bullet found its mark where he initially intended to put it. The Witch doctor fell to the floor dead. The amount of evidence collected after was more than enough to end suspicion and actually know for a fact the witch was the monster behind the killings, a lot of stuff linking to the deaths were recovered, she always kept an item belonging to the victims. The land behind the hut was a mass graveyard, people were shocked of the discovery the numbers of people that were killed were astounding, some sort of ritual was performed with them. The amount of animal remains is unfathomable. It was a gross, vile, and pure evil presence that lived there as no sane man could have done such atrocious killings to this scale, based on what was done there. Most of the details discovered were kept classified by the Israeli army and I could tell from Noam's expression that it disturbed him deeply of the finding they uncovered.

The next full moon came, and six days after the $5^{th}$ full moon a dead body was found. I know everyone thought that it was the witch, and it was obvious the witch too had been involved in a completely different killing spree which wouldn't have been discovered if it weren't for these mysterious deaths. Nobody knows why these killings are happening, who is doing it and how long it is going to continue. The mystery is still unsolved and every year six lives are lost in the first six full moons and bodies are found on the sixth day.

# Chapter 7
# Haunting in Lake View Resort

Time was around 10:30 pm signs of winter approaching was evident as a thick fog began engulfing the resort. I was spooked hearing Noam's story and felt the chill breeze blow in through the window, this caught my attention of the fog settling outside. Felt like I made a mistake dropping by that day in the resort as I began to feel a strong grip of fear take over me. I poured myself another drink and lit a joint. Ten years back when the resort was flourishing with business a young lady who was widowed met with her friends in the resort. It has been a month since she lost her husband, and her closest friends organized a fun trip to the resort. She was reluctant to come at first, but her friends were very concerned for her wellbeing. They wished to see her happy and jovial as she once was and insisted on a trip just to get her mind of her loss. After a lot of convincing she agreed, she arrived with her closest friend she knew from childhood, Mahmooda. The group arrived in two vehicles a total of six women all close friends to the widow.

    They have booked two queen suites overlooking the lake, and they shacked up together in threes in each room. The trip was planned for a total of seven days and six nights. They were engaged in taking long walks, swimming in the lake, enjoying long meals, relaxing in the sun, and even crying together to comfort their friend. Little did they know that on the $5^{th}$ day tragedy would strike again. The press came out with headlines reading White Widow's mysterious death. Hence forth the name stuck as the White Widow deaths. And later all hauntings in the lake resort were referred to as the White Widow hauntings. The day of her death, Riya woke up early in the morning she decided to go for a walk alone, this we know as she left a note for her friends. Since she decided to go alone many claimed she woke up with the intention of suiciding, but the cops claimed it was a freak accident. At 4:40 am she was seen leaving her room which was captured by the CCTV camera. She was later seen walking past the changing rooms which was also caught by the CCTV camera at around 5:15 am. Her friends woke up around 7:00 am, they saw the note she left behind. They were a bit worried but planned to give her space and so no one went in search of her. Since they did not know what time, she left they assumed she would be back for breakfast which they usually have at 8:30 am but she did not come by then. They then planned to walk towards the lake expecting to find her there as it was her favorite spot. When they arrived at the lake there was no sign of her, so they split up and went in several directions in search of her. By noon when they still haven't found her, they got worried, and they called the cops. The cops arrived and questioned each of the friends and several others in the resort, the cops informed the group of girls to relax and most probable they might expect her soon. She must be sitting somewhere to clear head they assumed. The cops told them that missing person report can be filed only after 24 hrs. They gave them their contact details and asked to contact the police if Riya was still missing after 24hrs.

24hrs later a missing person report was filed a few locals said they have seen her during early morning hours heading to the far end of the lake. Her body was recovered at the same spot, looked like she fell into the lake, at the far end of the lake the land was a bit raised and there was no shoreline. The water at this part is very deep and when she fell her feet were tangled with the weeds that grew in the lake. She died by drowning, her friends were in a shock, it was a very sad day. The case was not investigated further as there was no signs of struggle or bodily wounds from the postmortem. The tragedy shook the locals and the staff of the resort, there haven't been such an incident in their history, and it was the first of its kind. Then shortly after the infamous sighting and haunting of the white widow began.

There are stories of doors opening, windows opening all by themselves, voice of the woman crying from several locations in the resort, doorknobs turning a few have seen the white widow herself. Various papers covered stories of the haunting. People flooded in to experience these haunting but three years later two other deaths happened in similar fashion one in November and the other in December, the first was drowning of a teen boy in the lake and the other was an electrocution case of a woman in the bathtub. Then the papers came out with stories, with headlines that read, "White Widow deaths, Lake View home of the killer ghost, White Window the ghost killer." TV shows of the hauntings in the lake resort were aired, the owners were interviewed. Later the owners were accused of the killings which proved not to be true, but after the final tragedy less crowds visited the Lake

Resort. The reputation of the resort was destroyed, and it became a bad omen to visit the resort in the months of November and December and as years passed by more and more exaggerated stories were rumored around and slowly and gradually over the years fewer people came to the resort. Now the owners have put the property in the market for sale and a famous businessman was interested in the property. Due to disagreement in the price of the land and the resort the sale was not made. But many rumors are still going around, so nobody knows for a fact if negotiations are on-going or if the deal is completely of but the interested party the businessman is very keen on buying the property.

So now that you have the history of the resort, Noam had been calling me for several weeks to visit him. The incidents were happening at an increased frequency suddenly and he had been investigating this sudden increase in the hauntings. He would hear windows break, a woman's scream at some nights, sightings of the white widow, one night a certain part of the resort caught on fire mysteriously and that area had no camera. Incidents of stones being thrown at the watchman's cabin happened more than once, Noam knew something fishy was going on and he needed help and I have no clue why he thought of me. I wanted no part of this madness but since I heard the resort would be sold soon and hearing of plans of demolishing the resort was also rumored, out of an impulse to experience old nostalgic times I spend there made me change my plans to layover that night. Fearing that the place would be changed, and I wouldn't be able to experience the resort as I remembered it, my heart tricked my mind to staying over.

I was particularly back for Romina a house maid who came to change the sheet every morning, I have changed the sheets with Romina several times over the years. I was one of her favorite guests she liked visiting, so I believed, her shift was in the morning, and I felt like changing the sheets for one last time with Romina. Somewhere deep inside me I knew this would be my last visit to the resort, I was growing tired of all the thrill seeking, drinking, the drugs I was yearning for more in my life. I wanted my adventures to begin in a different direction I wanted to build my life back up. I have been trapped in these useless thrill-seeking ways which was destroying me. I knew I had to address my addictions one day. As time went on my usage kept on increasing and was getting out of control. Recently over the past few months I had this strong urge to change. Since then, a new pattern of behavior emerged in me, as I was planning to quit, I started using it more and more and procrastinated consistently when it came to quitting and kept shifting the date further out. I was buying time to stay addicted, with the hope that if I used enough of it, I will be satisfied one day and that day I will quit, to stop my addictions. Felt like I just added more fuel to the fire, now it's just a matter of time if I would really stop or fall to my addictions.

My dinner arrived the duck roast was my weakness, so I devoured the roasted bird in minutes as I was hungry. Noam looked and me and asked, "Are you scared?" I looked back at him and said, "Should I be, because if I should be, I will leave now." He laughed and said, "It's okay to be scared." Noam suspected that the recent events were staged, it was difficult for him to catch them because he was outnumbered, and they were very careful and well planned. The duck disappeared from my plate and filled in my belly, it was delicious as the first time I tried it, I ordered another one thinking if I will ever have the chance again, I will miss this duck roast. I lit a joint and poured myself a drink, I was on my 7$^{th}$ double and now I started to get my courage back. At this point I would fight anybody and with the weed I was in a very wonderful place mentally. I began to feel that my last drink was a bit too much and I should I have stopped but instead I gulped it down and poured myself another.

Noam and I decided to look around, I headed to the east wing and Noam the west wing, we swept every room checking for any suspicious activity. I just kept kicking at the door and moved on. I remember reaching the White Widows room and letting it be, I didn't not want to wake her up nor disturb her slumber, she must rest cannot risk her waking. *I am completely drunk, why did I plan to come here,* I thought to myself. I should have drove back to my room. My breathing was heavy, and I wished the night could end soon. I started walking back to Noam's cabin. I knew I shouldn't be drinking anymore but the first thing I did was pour myself another drink, Noam was nowhere to be seen I finished my drink and headed out again in search of Noah. As I walked out of the cabin, I decided I'd have another drink and I went back and quickly had another drink and set out to search for Noam. I went straight to the west wing, I found nobody there, except for the couple who were staying for the night. The only other place he could be was at the lake, I knew it was a bad idea venturing in those parts of the resort at this time of night. But when your drunk anything is possible, and I stumbled towards the lake without making any noise. There was no light, and I was finding my way through the dark hoping to find Noam. Approaching the lake at the far end I could see a bonfire and group of people standing around the fire. The sensible guy in me said not to shout and get their attention, the drunk guy in me shouted out even before I could talk any sense into him. My shout was followed by utter silence, I saw a lot of shadows move around the fire, the group gathered were trying to identify the source of the sound, and then the shadows moved fast and disappeared into the darkness, I knew I was in trouble cause those shadows didn't react like I sacred them off it felt like they were threatened and ready for confrontation. Then I started to hear several voices, screams and shouts coming from that direction and then and there I knew the shit had officially hit the ceiling. I began running as fast as I could back to Noam's cabin. Felt impossible to lift my feet and run, gravity seemed to have dialed its intensity up a hundred-fold and I barely felt myself moving. I was scared to death and panicking to the extend I forecasted every probability of shitting my pants.

So, while I was heading towards the resort, Noam heard my shout and he started making his way towards me. The couples who were staying over for the night was frightened and were planning to get away from the resort. Moments before I put all these events into motion, on the far end of the lake around the spot the White widow tragedy took place a small group of around 11 people gathered around a fire that was lit by their leader. They were hired to stage hauntings in the resort. While they grouped around the fire to discuss that nights haunting episodes, their leader gave them the routine to follow of the several scenarios they have planned to execute. They were a very sly cunning group of people who have successful pulled this job off for the past couple of months without being caught. Noam's hunch was right at the end, their sole purpose was to orchestrate these events to scare the customers and staff of the property, to portray to the public that the land was cursed.

Everything went according to their plan, until that night to their bad luck someone witnessed their meeting and out of sudden panic the leader ordered his gang to track the witness, me, down. I wasn't sure what they planned to do with me but anyway one thing was sure they did not intend to bless me with a good night, and they wanted to catch me to do bad stuff I guessed. I was running like a mad man and the weed and the alcohol in me, made me feel like I weight a ton or I though the gravity was playing a very nasty trick on me, I could barely move but I had to, so I was running like a mad man, literally trying to move my frozen legs to safety as soon as possible. Unlike the hallucinations I had during my time with the shaman, what was happening at that time wasn't real. But now these were real people after my ass, and not knowing what they'd do to me made the whole experience even more terrifying. What a week I thought to myself, I kept cursing myself and calling myself an idiot repeatedly. To make matters worse the lights went off everywhere, I tripped and fell to the ground, I was breathing like I ran a 100mtr dash, I had to be brave now and was faking the brave attitude very badly. Normally at these times when I'm scared and petrified, I think of Arnold Schwarzenegger. Yes, Arnold Schwarzenegger the Actor from every action movie in the '90s, I pretend to be Arnold from the movie *Predator: Fighting the Alien*. I always thought if I sounded and moved like him, I would scare the threat away. I once pretended to be like Arnold when I got into a fight when I was young, and it scared the other guy off, I'd shout and scream and make noises like Arnold fighting the predator and move aggressively like I suddenly got possessed by Arnold himself. This was when I was a kid but while I lay on the ground there shitting bricks with a group of people coming to get me the Arnold in me awakened once again.

I could see Noam approaching from a distance and he had no clue I turned into Arnold. Noam was worried something happened to me, I was on the ground trying to get up, barely able to stand, making weird noises which he did not relate to in anyway. "Are you okay," he shouted, and I was drunk and scared and shouted back at him, "Get to the chopper."

"Get down," babbling like a true drunk. Noam clearly saw I was drunk out of my mind, he lifted me up on his shoulders and carried me to his cabin. I continued babbling, managed to get a couple of dialogues from terminator as well. Noam was beginning to worry; he had never seen me in this state, and I always could handle any amount of liquor I drank. My behavior was unusual and very unlike myself, he placed me on his couch calmed me down, once I began to relax but still drunk my speech slurring, I told him about what I saw. He was relieved I was alright, and he handed me a bottle of water, just then there was knocking on the door. The couples were standing outside looking very worried and scared, Noam explained to them that everything is fine and there is nothing to worry and persuaded them not to leave at this time of the night. They too joined me on the couch, my roasted duck was sitting on the table, and I ate that duck in no time.

My stomach full and feeling a little better I reached out to the bottle when Noam stopped me. "Enough for you," he said and took the bottle away from my hand and locked it in his shelf. "You have a problem, son, and you should seriously think of quitting," he said. Noam called the police fearing an attack, howling sounds emerged from outside. When the howling stopped stones were hurled at us, all the windows were shattered. Noam got his gun and made three warning shots and shouted that if they attacked us, he would shoot. Once again silence filled the air and they stopped throwing stones, they were trying to get us to leave the cabin. Few moments later they started screaming and shouting this time they slowly emerged from behind the tress, they were all wearing mask. They just stood there surrounding the cabin, now, we were trapped inside the cabin.

Noam asked us to stay still and stay low on the floor, Noam loaded his gun he was ready to take them down. Several minutes later they started throwing rocks that were set on fire, we kept putting them of as and when they came in through the window. Our only hope was for the cops to reach us as early as possible. Noam started firing at them and they stopped once again. This went on for a while and Noam would stop them by firing at them. Then something strange happened a woman's scream was heard coming from inside the east wing. The first scream got the con artist to stop throwing stones and with the second scream they all got a little scared. Noam slowly got up and looked outside the window and noticed the masked people around 11 of them were all looking towards the east wing and when he looked in that direction, he could not believe what he saw and sat back down.

I asked him what happened as he seemed like he saw a ghost and ghost did he see; the white window was walking down the east wing we all could see her in a white dress as she walked along the east wing corridor. Each window flung open as she passed by them, and the windows flung open banging against the wall shattering the glasses. None of us could believe what we were looking at and we all were in disbelief to what we witnessed. I sobered the second I saw her, it was like she was gliding through the air, and she had her face turned towards the people attacking us. Felt like I was in a James Wan horror movie, could this be even true I looked at Noam and his reaction too was the same. He took the rum bottle out of the cupboard and drank a mouthful; he then passed the bottle towards me, and I emptied it. None of us knew how to react to this situation. I took this as a warning to leave the resort, the group outside started throwing stones at the white window, when the stones did nothing, they set the building on fire. Mean time we got out of the cabin and escaped to the car park. The couple got into their car and Noam, and I got into mine. We had no idea where the maid and the chef were, we drove off together to the police station where we all made a statement of what we witnessed.

After that night's events the Resort was completely shut down. Noam returned to his country where he spent the rest of his life with family. He died four years after the incident, the maid, and the chef from that night managed to escape on foot, they later got married and started a small restaurant, they still claim to see the white widow by the lake and in the premises of the resort. The couple that spend the night there returned to the city where they worked, and we meet up every year to remember our experience. I drove back to the city after giving the police my statement and never came back to that place.

# Chapter 8
# Weather Forecast – Depression

I was sitting in my cubicle at the office remembering my time with Rahu, the shaman and Noam. I had enough of these adventures, in most of my trips to these places I always thought to myself that I would find answer's that would help me in my life. I just mentioned two stories, but I had a hell a lot of experiences out with random people in risky situations. I always felt that I would find solutions or answers for my life if I went on for more of these trips I would be cured of my misery. Though they were exciting at the moments I experienced them when I got back, I would feel low, empty, and dejected. These experiences did not motivate me nor inspire me but rather were an excuse for me to escape my true reality so I could indulge in overwhelming quantities of alcohol and drugs. Nothing felt right, felt like everything was off and I was completely out of line within my-self. A whirlpool of destructive emotions aggressively expressed itself felt like I had no control over myself. Felt like a maniac was on the driving seat while I was gagged, tied, and thrown in the trunk of my sub-conscious. All this time all I wanted was to be normal like the rest of the people around me, but I always felt like I never fit in, felt like a fish out of water.

I drank when I was bored, I drank when I felt depressed, drank when I felt like I was not good enough, I drank because I felt like a failure, I drank to feel some emotion. I felt numb, drained, and felt only pain. The pain, where do I start the pain which I just couldn't let go off or heal, the epicenter of all my problems, a void in me that could not be filled up with any amount of alcohol, weed, mushrooms or cough syrup. Felt like it got bigger and bigger each time I tried to numb it with my medication. The constant thrill-seeking behaviors grew and now I had a large appetite, coming back to work was torture. I couldn't keep still no part of me was still I wanted to get out and do something and that something always started with alcohol. I couldn't feel joy until I had a joint or a pint, anything that numbed the pain and made me feel alive. I loved exploring more creative ways to get high. I would stay up drinking all night and hoping that the night would never end. There were many other things I wished to do, like get into shape, save money and be successful in life, travel around the world, write a book, start a business and so much more. But every time I tried moving in that direction that encouraged growth in a positive direction I couldn't go far. I would start a hundred things without being able to finish it.

The only thing I ended up doing was to drink and smoke weed most of the time. There were several occasions I would decide to drive back to my room after work or after grocery shopping, but I would end up in a pub drinking. Things got out of hand, I didn't want to go back to my room at all, all I wanted was to party all night, that's when I started spending nights in hotels with pros for company. I would try to change my ways daily, but I failed and failed and failed repeatedly. Every time I tried to change for good the darkness would suck me back deeper; I had to resist and take a tremendous amount of effort to stir my life into the right direction and every time I resisted from these dark habits it would fight back with greater power. It really felt like someone else was living inside me.

I was never like this, I was the obedient son, the first time I took a drug or drank alcohol was to understand the fascination behind it, I wondered why my father couldn't give it up, I had to know what he found in these substances. I had to know why he was so addictive to them, in the early stages I wondered how anybody could be controlled by any substance. The whole idea itself was rubbish as I felt and knew for a fact that I will never be an addict as much as I consumed it. I was young, healthy and no matter how much I consumed during those ages I never had the need to do them again the next day. This was a habit that was built over time and my doses kept increasing. After a life changing breakup combined with my failure to find the job I desired, along with being kicked out of the house by my dad, sparked something in me. Yes, I was shocked and in disbelief when my then girlfriend left, I did break my heart in a million ways, yes, but it wasn't that I couldn't handle it, I knew I fucked up my chances on getting the right job and I knew I could apply for jobs again, and my dad kicking me out of home too was for the right reasons he wanted me to stand on my own two feet. I understood all this and took all of this positively but then my bad luck began.

No matter what I did to get back up and stir my life in the right direction I was rejected, doors shut down on me, I was not only rejected but also discouraged. I once had an interviewer tell me that I will never become an Engineer after a two-hour interview asking me every damn thing in the history of Engineering itself. I would have applied to at least 8000 jobs in a span of six years, attended several online tests to finally be rejected in the final interview. I eventually had to get a job in an industry I had no idea about, I had tremendous pressure and the volume of work was so overwhelming overbearing. I was literally doing the work of several people. And as years went by it became more and more evident that the possibility to work in the industry, I was interested in was closing rapidly. I was stuck at my horrible job that paid me peanuts which would have helped if I were a monkey. My first job was at a call center, which shut down the 3$^{rd}$ day I joined, then worked as a market analyst for a newly launched hypermarket and I was send to the field to roam around malls and houses collecting information for the analyst. I left that job as I couldn't even afford to pay for rent with that job. Finally, I ended up working for a construction company as a buyer which paid enough money.

I was in a hurry to get successful fast to save my mother and sister from my father. But the harder I tried the more I was rejected and when all my efforts were going in vain and not able to understand what I was doing wrong my drinking and drugs usage exploded out of control. And I hated myself for it, but I couldn't control myself. My dreams were becoming distant, and the addictions became my reality. The depression I was in lasted a decade, I was becoming someone I always feared I would become, the last thing I wanted was to become my father. My aim was the other direction where I made money made my mother proud supported them well. But I was spiraling out of control, and I never blamed anyone but myself for it. I withdrew from everyone, as I had to get to the bottom of this, change, and achieve what I wanted to achieve. There was no turning back now, I was completely prepared to put myself through anything to get there.

I read everything there was to read about depression, I met several shrinks to get the bottom of my problem. When I was unhappy with a shrink, I would move on to another and then another. I met them while I was sober and most of the times when I was drunk. I once remember meeting a counsellor who at the last minute changed her schedule by two hours so I obviously had to kill time until she was ready to have my session and so I went to the nearest pub gulped down eight pints arrived 20 mins early smoked a joint in the car park, and finished the shrooms while I waited at the reception for her to call me in. The receptionist was very concerned when I started talking with the water dispenser as it transformed into an angel and started conversing with me. When I was finally invited in for my session the councilor clearly could see I was under the influence of several substances. I couldn't stop talking to her about how much I loved her office and the changes she made, the shrooms were doing its work and all I could see was a variety of colors which seemed like wet paint flowing into each other and making new colors I was completely appreciating her for her taste. It didn't stop there I told her I was experiencing an awakening and the heavens keep sending angels to me. I told her about the angel waiting in the reception room, and then somewhere between these conversations I forgot I was attending my counselling session and started removing my clothes thinking I was in the company of a pro with whom I was about to have epic sex.

I woke over several hours later in a bed, in the adjacent room, and the councilor walked in and broke the news of my antics, she did not throw me out but instead made it a point I had my session compulsorily that day forward and she would be putting my name in as one of her top priority clients. I was asked to attend AA and SAA meeting, she referred me to two people one in AA and one in SAA to help me deal with my urges. If you're not familiar with the terms AA, it stands for Alcoholic Anonymous a support group for Alcoholics and other was for sex addicts. Now little did she know that I was the kind of devil that ended by sleeping with my AA partner Racheal who I was meant to call if I was having drinking urges. Racheal a divorcee on her early thirties had no clue I was also a sex addict; the AA meeting would usually be on Friday mornings, and I would pick her up from her apartment. I would get busy with her while I picked her up from her apartment, before we entered the meeting in my car and then after the meeting in the women washroom. After my AA meeting after dropping Racheal, I would meet Pablo an Italian architect with a severe sex addiction in a pub and we would drink and share stories of our experiences and then attend the SAA meeting at 4:00 pm.

I couldn't stop myself from doing any of these things and every time I did it, I would feel like this is how it's meant to be. This is how I feel naturally inside me, I would justify that doing all this is my path and how the universe itself wants me to be. Anytime I tried taking responsibility for my actions I would feel that pain inside my heart and think that it is the sign from the heavens for me to do whatever I planned to do. The urges could strike at any moment, and I would act immediately out of impulse without having the ability to stop and think if it was right. To be honest I was tired of being the good son, I was tired of people's opinions of how I should live and conduct my life. I wanted to create and experience life as I wanted it and what I was doing then felt like it was meant to be and the things I should be doing. I always felt bad, angry, and felt deep resentment towards myself when I used to get up sober, I hated myself and felt very low and depressed after these episodes. I was scared that I couldn't control myself at all.

Every time Rachel called me when she felt like she was about to break and drink I would rush to her place and yes, seduce her. And every time Pablo felt he was about to break and end up fucking a stranger I would end up drinking with him in a pub. Now Racheal, Pablo and I went to the same shrink, over a period somewhere between six and eight months. The shrink began to see similar patterns of my behavior emerging in Racheal and Pablo. Somehow Racheal did not relapse back to drinking but she had developed the need for sex instead of alcohol and Pablo for alcohol instead of sex. She began suspecting that she might have made a mistake, but Racheal never disclosed anything about our encounters outside of AA and Pablo outside of SAA. Racheal and Pablo had been through years of therapy and showed excelled recovery in their respective addictions and over time when they showed excellent progress, they were often asked by the shrink to help people like me who were still struggling deep in their addictions. Rachael and Pablo have helped several people like that over the years and helped many people recover.

This was until I came into their lives, Now Pablo's drinking started building up and he would always invite me couple of times a week to catch up with a drink. Both Pablo and Racheal were unaware that I was undergoing my so-called recovery with alcohol and sex. Meantime Racheal started having more encounters with more and more people. I used to meet Racheal several times a week and couple of times some days. It got so bad that Racheal would call me in the middle of work sometimes and I would end up driving to her apartment blow her mind off the roof and then come back to work. Eventually, she started developing emotional problems that made her feel the same way she felt while she used to drink. She finally broke the news with our shrink who immediately called Pablo who immediately confirmed about his drinking and his meetings with me on several occasions. The bubble burst, I was completely exposed, I received a message one fine day asking me to come in for a surprise session. I was completely unaware that the shrink found out. When I walked into her office, I was surprised to see Rachael and Pablo, I wanted to run away but I was trapped. I thought they were going to shout and blame me but instead they all came over and hugged me. We had a group session mainly feedback on my behavior towards Racheal and Pablo and how I managed to break their sobriety which they maintained for years. After they finished talking, they were asked to leave, and I was alone with the shrink, after we spoke, she increased my sessions with her and put me through an intensive recovery program for my recovery.

But that was the last time I ever went to meet her or any shrink ever. Months later I got a call from Pablo who called me to tell he was getting married to Racheal. Yes, I managed to get these two people together, once again. They have organized a special party just for me, which was just the three of us as Racheal was worried, I might sleep with someone she knew, and Pablo was worried I might end up drinking all the alcohol. Anyway, they are living a very happy life now and are expecting a child. This was the last time I saw Racheal and Pablo, they always called to check in and invited me a couple of times for dinner, but I kept avoiding them. Not sure why, once I feel like the natural cycle of our relationship has come to an end then I just don't keep in touch irrespective of what the actual reality is. This is how I generally feel with most relationships, I just move on and never keep in touch. Never knew why I do that but guess it's just the way I am.

Deep in my sub-conscious I knew it had to do with me being accepted, as I am uniquely different with my challenges, predominantly it was deep concern I carried for being judged. But despite all these things deep inside me I always wanted only one thing, that was to change my life, but I felt so trapped and out of control I didn't know how to reach there. Every day I looked for answers and methods to be able to change, but I failed, again, again and again. Even if I was in a great deal of pain and disappointment with myself, I always held on to hope I always lived optimistically that one day I would truly change, I always felt like I was being guided by some mysterious force invisible to the eye, but heartfelt. I always felt like I was protected and even at times when shit had hit the ceiling and life was above to kick me in the ass, I would emerge out of the situation safe and soundly alive.

Even if I was depressed, drunk or high I never missed work and worked my ass off. I never stopped searching for ways for me to improve, I tried different ways to make more money but always failed to make much progress out of bad fucking luck or things not working out in my favor. I have lived to see friends become enemies and enemies become friends, I seen many get married and have children, the world seemed to be progressing well and taking everyone else along on its ride while I was left behind on that station of progress for reasons I couldn't figure out. I was getting tired of it all, trying to control myself, trying to make things happen that were clearly out of my control, trying to pull out a miracle when it felt like I was cursed. I remember getting tickets for a Metallica concert and nearly 25,000 people turned up. I was with my friends having a good time and after the concert I had to catch a cab, which I shared with a married couple who wanted to take me home with them. I was way too drunk and just wanted to get home, and the only reason I agreed to get in the cab was I got to split the cash for the cab, and we were also heading the same direction.

But somewhere on the way the wife had her hands down my pants and kept insisting me to join them. What should have been a great experience based on all what was happening in my life at that time didn't feel so. I woke up feeling sick to my stomach the next day scared and frightened of what I was becoming, have I dangerously taken myself to far away from my sanity. The fact that I left with them didn't bother me, what bothered me was that I didn't want to leave with them and yet went through with it. I could no longer listen to that quiet voice in my head that always tries to save me from doing something that I would regret and cannot be undone. I feared that I have rebelled against myself to an extend I would not listen to the voice of reason inside me and risk my life for cheap thrills that only hurt me more. I was worried, I was not okay, I needed help, it would be under these circumstances I would try to run away on a trip to get away from feeling my emotions. But I was tired of those trips too because I began to understand no matter where I ran my mind is still going to be the same and I would be feeling the same emotions that I am trying to avoid instead of addressing them. I wondered why am I like this? Why am I behaving like this? Is this how my life is going to be? Will I ever turn my life around? I can't be just this I knew this in my heart and now I also knew I have a problem, a problem I couldn't find a solution too. It was very important to me that I never get help from my family or friends I had to overcome this by myself, and I wanted it that way for me. I didn't regret what I have done, but I was torn apart from the fact that I was not doing things that really mattered in my life, I was tormenting myself for not overcoming my trials and I didn't want anybody's help but mine. I felt nobody would understand me and if it came to saving me it must be only me, I no longer trusted nor wanted anyone to come fix me. I was done with their ways, I was done with their opinions was done with their comparisons, I was done with their advises. What hurt the most was when finally, I had complete control over my life and I could change anything and achieve anything I couldn't do it, somehow it felt like I became how everyone would have judged me or expected me to become and I hated that.

I am a very optimistic guy and I pursue all my dreams as much as I can, but now it's been a while since I have achieved anything. The direction my life was going felt scary and seemed very predictable. *I felt like the Gods knew that if they lifted this curse or bad luck out of my way, I would have achieved whatever I dreamt off, maybe they don't want all these things for me,* I thought. The apple didn't fall far away from tree, and now the apple lay on the ground rotting in need of some serious divine intervention. I needed a miracle to turn this ship around and strike gold in every voyage I set sail towards. I felt let down and confused, I knew I had to change, I knew I had to do something so brilliant to finally be where I wanted to be and feel like I wanted to feel. I was exhausted and I needed rest, the time was 5:30 am and I had to go to the office at 8:00 am. Once I reached my room after the debauchery with the married couple, I slept for like an hour and turned up to the office smelling like a mini bar. I worked until noon until my manager broke the ice and told me to go home and take rest. Instead of going home I drove straight to a pub drank a couple of pints and ended up visiting a pro.

My insides were in a total state of rebellion and anarchy, there was no way of talking sense to this person running the show. I had to find a whole other creative way to handle my compulsions. But just when I have decided to change the devil sends someone to destroy any progress I have made and re-invented havoc inside me, so that I fell flat on my face. After the incident from the concert, I managed to stay sober for a month, I was doing good, it was tough I hated being sober, it was a lot of energy to keep the sobriety up when one fine day I ran into my ex-shrink, I tried getting away, but she cornered me at the escalator, we were at a mall for different reasons, and this run in happened by pure chance. She immediately put me at easy and invited me for a snack at the food court. At the food court she told me it was okay if I didn't want to see her anymore and expressed genuine concern for my wellbeing. I told her I was sober for a month, and I have been doing it with a great deal of effort. She congratulated me and told me I was doing the right thing and encouraged my progress. This was the last time I met her.

After having met my ex-shrink, I felt a little confident and happy for my sobriety and I felt like I could do anything. In a happy mood I got in the car and started driving I meant to drive back to my room, but I was passing familiars roads that lead to my favorite pub. Thought I'd drop in and tell everyone that I have quit for good, and they will not be seeing me again. I dropped the car at the hotel valet and walked into the pub, the moment the bartender saw me and even before I could open my mouth to speak, he handed me a pint. And even without a thought like a reflex I lifted the pint towards my mouth and the moment the first drop of alcohol hit my tongue it felt like heaven. I have the will to stop now I said to myself and another voice said maybe this one pint, later that evening on my sixth pint I told the bartender I was quitting for good after this, then after my tenth pint I ordered my eleventh. I was singing with the band, joking with the regulars at the pub, ordered calamari and the twelfth pint. By that time the bar tender was already joking about my stories of quitting, pigs need to fly upside down added the manager for this guy to quit. The bouncer added even if no one came but him the pub would still run-on profit.

I stopped after my sixteenth pint and the time was 2:00 am, instead of going home I booked a room in the hotel as I was clearly drunk and called a pro to finish off the night with a bang. The next day I woke up in an utter state of panic and the guilt came rushing back a voice in my head whispered why? Why? WHY? You deviated from the plan again why? I stumbled out of bed took a shower paid the bill and started driving back to the office feeling utterly disgusted at myself all over again. The whole day was horrible, I had a ton of work, and more work was dumped onto my table. I had 1000 calls to attend, meetings in between. At the end of the day, I was exhausted and went straight to bed. I lay on my bed cursing why I went out in the first place; I should have stayed in my room. I immediately banned myself from going out anymore until I felt it was okay for sure for me to step out. I planned to spend the rest of my days only at the office working and then back to my room after working out in the gym. This was the plan I kept saying to myself, I was ready and I'm ready to make this change. I was constantly in the look out when I will screw up next, because it came to that point, I had to focus all my energy on myself to not screw up. But later that night I ended up leaving to the city and yes, I drank once again, I drank the next day and the day after and then weekend came and the only thing I had to do was drink again.

Depression, what a fascinating state of mind it is, do animals get depressed? I'm curious, do plants get depressed? I wonder, because of all the living beings on planet earth the homo sapiens wreak havoc upon themselves and their loved ones when depression hits them. Homo sapiens become a different animal altogether when they suffer from mental illness, so despite us being the superior life form with all the intelligence, that create wonders on this planet we have equal capacity to destroy, which is a dangerous power gifted to the homo sapiens. If they are not mentally sound and soulfully connected for the better good of the planet, they are no good to the planet. And due to the intelligence possessed by them the planet and all its beings have no greater threat than the homo sapiens. They possess equal power to create and destroy, we were truly made in the image of God and have been gifted God like power. Imagine if God had depression, we all are screwed right, we would not even stand a chance against such a power, no form of defense could protect us and no strategy would work against him, we are doomed if he got depressed, we would not be able to survive without his mercy.

Mental health is no joke, it must be considered as one of the biggest problems for mankind to tackle. Governments should spend more on this matter and help heal broken minds than invest on military needs. Maybe if we all healed completely, we would stop fighting each other, there would be no necessity to build atom bombs and fighter jets. All that money spend for destruction could be used for other major concerns. But mankind shows capacity to change only at the 11$^{th}$ hour when destruction is right at the corner and their lives are at threat. And I was no different, little did I know about the consequences I was about to face while I abused my body with various chemicals.

I began to understand my father better, maybe he too was depressed or maybe he was hiding so much pain within himself. Maybe that's why he drank himself to death, what killed him wasn't the alcohol, it was a broken heart. I felt sorry and deeply saddened as I never met a man like him in my life. He was so intelligent, the most intelligent man I ever met, handsome, charming with a brilliant sense of humor. He was like a magnet when he put on his charm, a very brilliant surgeon, he was awesome, as awesome as, you can imagine how a man should be made. And it always perplexed me how of all the people that he would fall prey to addiction. How could my champion, who I knew for a fact, the toughest man in the world, be dissolved by alcohol? This curiosity to understand him motivated me to indulge in things I didn't know that would eventually put me through hell, but as I went through hell I understood my father, I felt deeply sad and angry at myself for not being a kind, compassionate son, I loved him to bits, yet I hurt him a lot, this tore me apart but I didn't know of it then cause I couldn't feel anything. This I learnt much later, the true emotions I had for my father. I no longer was ashamed of my situation, if I did this to understand my dad, I made another promise that I will overcome this terrible illness that has been slowing me down, I will not only overcome it and defeat the beast, but I will conquer the world for him. I wanted him to feel so proud that it would set him free, I wanted to give him so much love, respect, and honor, by dedicating my life's success as his success.

Yes, I was drinking while I pondered on these thoughts, but I meant it, and I was willing to go to any lengths, at any cost and through any amount of pain to hold his name high cause he deserved it, my father was more than a drunk or alcoholic, he was a miracle that failed to happen and now it was time for the world to see him in his true colors.

# Chapter 9
# Fallen Prince

I have many fond memories of my father, he taught me how to swim, ride my bicycle, he took me fishing and hunting, he took me for his walks in the coffee estate, he taught me to drive, to tuck my shirt and above all he taught me to be a man. I'd say my father was great at being a father, he just happened to do it differently when he started falling to alcohol. He was hard on me and spared no mercy when it came to learning lessons that were required in life, he was tough when he wanted to toughen me but the rest of the time, he was my best friend. There was no topic we haven't discussed, we debated, we disagreed, but I always listened. His insights and philosophy in life captivated me and I admired him. He was my mentor, my guide, and I felt proud to have him as my father. There was nothing to be afraid of when he was beside me because he was truly a lion at heart.

My treasured memories I have of him is the time we spend alone, he used to take me out most evenings to meet all my uncles at a local pub back in my hometown. Where they all would sit around in a long table drinking and I used to oversee him interact with them. He was a man's man, kind of a guy, nobody could bullshit him, his mind was sharp as a laser. I loved hanging around him and I would follow him everywhere and he always spoke to me like I'm one of his guys, he'd become my father only to discipline me. His behavior towards me started changing gradually over the years as his drinking got worse. His appetite for alcohol would exponentially grow over the years and he behaved like he was running out of time. The older I got the worse his drinking got the only things we would speak and advise me was on life, the responsibilities I had to lead the family, where the important documents were filed. Each year it felt like he was handing over the mantle to me, and he got tougher and tougher on me so I could live up to the task when the time came.

As his drinking got worse my mother would go to bed early and keep his dinner on the table. The truth was he would start abusing my mother, by yelling at her. Complaining, calling her insulting names, attacking her mentally so she would go to bed. My sister would already be in her room as she was tired off all the fighting and never wanted to be the reason for our father to shout and blame our mother. This behavior grew more consistently over the years and eventually they would just stay in their rooms. At this time, he would talk to me, in the beginning he would tell me a lot of how the world is and how the people are in the world and how I should behave and act. He always encouraged me to aim for the stars and never settle for anything which is less that what I have dreamt off. He told me that he's only got a small part to play in my life and what I make out of my life is entirely up to me. He told me that he can only support me but it's me who will have to face trials and challenges life throws at me. It's me, who will have to climb the mountains I'm meant to climb, fights the battles in my mind and weather the storms that may come.

"I want you to grow a real pair of testicles," he would say. "Stop being a mama's boy, you got a dick for Christ's sake, quit being a pussy son." I would always ask him, "Why do you drink so much, isn't there any other way, why are you putting yourself through all this misery and pain, don't you want to be happy?" Always and always, he replied, "This is who I am, this is how I want to live, and this is how I want to die." He deeply loved my mother this I knew, and only years later did I understand the reason why he abused her so much, was only because he was angry and frustrated with his own self that he couldn't provide nor live up to be the man she truly deserved, she was a constant reminder of his failures and this hurt him, he never wanted her to leave his side at the same time he couldn't stop his drinking because it's all he wanted to do and he knew it wasn't fair for my mother. This failure to be the better man for her hurt him deeply and made him hurt her in ways he never should have because in his head there was no other way for him to stop her from leaving. This guilt and pain within him ate into his soul and since he already decided on continuing his path of destruction, he destroyed everything great and wonderful about himself. You can only treat others as you treat yourself. He abused himself so much to such a great extend he forgot what it was to love himself, since he felt only hate, and anger within him this is what he gave out to my mother and us kids.

As years passed by my late-night talks with my father gradually ended and when it did it was almost like he had given up altogether on himself. That's when our fights started, he would provoke me, kept repeating the same things again and again and again, he would ridicule me, call me a good for nothing. He distanced himself from me it felt like he was preparing me to become someone, I was yet to realize it, but he saw something in me. I stayed patient; it took every inch of my strength to resist myself from losing control. I was still in school, and he was still my father and I loved him, and I couldn't understand why he was doing all this. Why was he trying to abandon us? This is how it felt. As time went on, he was advancing into his addiction and the change in him was drastic, he retreated completely into himself, it was like he had a plan, but he wouldn't tell anybody. It got unbearable when he would start fights and keep repeating things and I cannot stop the emphasizing on the repetition on certain things, it was exhausting to the point of madness. My father used to hurt my mother physically, how could someone who loved her so much do such a thing like that. He had to do so I guess, because he knew within himself if it was up to her to leave, she would have and so he had to control her mentally and terrorize her, so she'll stay, without her he was completely lost. But my mother stayed with him despite it all, and she would have stayed until he tore her apart piece by piece. Their bond or love they had, I never understood, how could someone inflict so much pain on someone he loved so much, he couldn't live without her by his side and at the same time couldn't stop himself from hurting her, and how can someone go through all that abuse from someone who, she knew, loved her, but all she could feel was pain because of the love she had for him, how could she take all that and stay?

It was my mother who always told us kids that whatever my father is going through was an illness and it is not the real man he is. She kept telling us this all through the years, she always had hope in her heart he would change, she always held her tears back in front of her kids as much as she could. But the real horrible years came and the tears that flowed from her eyes would have filled oceans, she prayed and prayed to God for her husband. She woke up every day, doing things beyond her best to make a home, if it wasn't for her, we all would have been doomed. Her love kept him alive, and he survived by consuming into her soul drinking all the energy out of her like a hungry vampire leaving her emotionless and numb with pain. A man isn't strong and there is nothing stronger than a woman, we all survived because of her. We all had a light in those dark years as she became our light. From her I learnt forgiveness, from her I learnt what it really means to love, from her I learnt what it means to sacrifice everything for nothing in return.

She always kept reminding, us kids, that our father was suffering from an illness, and it would be wrong to judge him for he is not in his senses, it's the alcohol that's making him do all this and he needs our support and help. That's when I started paying more attention to my father I would listen to him, I heard his pain empathized with him but the beating he gave my mother had to stop. It was the summer of 1999, and I was getting into high school after the summer vacation. As always, the vacations were gloomy, depressing and everyday felt like a new way to fight and hurt, and hate each other. Couldn't keep the TV on for long cause it's in the living room where my father sits to drink, and he hated the TV being on. Couldn't go out and play for long cause we have curfews to be kept. So being stuck in a space with an alcoholic who expresses anger and aggression all day and all night is a lot to take. Sometimes it would be silly stuff and my father would explode into a rage and he could start yelling at my mother, and one of those day being trapped with him and being frustrated myself, he got into a fight with my mother over something so silly, my sister ran into her room, and I was sitting in the living room where the fight broke out. My mother yelled back at my father, and he got up and slapped my mother so hard she fell on the floor. I don't know what came over me, but the next minute I remember was me standing and my father on floor, I saw that look in his eyes, he was shocked, and he never expected it, nor did I mean to do it. I slapped him so hard on his face he fell over and looked back at me, I still remember the look on his face, he was in disbelief, he couldn't believe that I would ever do this to him because he always thought I was a harmless guy, But I felt the pain he felt it wasn't the slap it was the emotional blow I gave him. Everything changed that day and he never ever laid a finger on my mother again and then on its was complete mind games.

That was the first time I struck him, I did not feel on top of the world, I did not feel like my testicles grew in girth I felt the pain he felt. It left like I slapped myself, I felt so broken and hurt I loved this man, I respected this man, he was everything to me, he was my hero. Our relationship drastically changed after that it was the beginning of an enmity that started growing over the years. I had to do certain things of a similar fashion over the years to control him when he would go overboard with his drinking. The once loving charming man was completely gone, before me was a stranger in my father's body. He became someone I could not recognize anymore; I knew I lost my father then; do you know how hard it is to love someone so much and be in a position to do things you don't want to do but your forced to do it because of the situation. Can you even begin to understand the pain to have a father you love so much, fall into addiction so deep that it changes him to an extend he behaves like you're his sore enemy, do you know the pain of being the son who he literally can recognize but treated you like an emotional punching bag. The pain of still loving him after all that and seeing him deteriorate while he strongly kept alienating me felt like a thousand deaths. This was the same way my mother and sister felt too, we felt helpless the only thing we could do is sit and watch him destroy himself.

My mother kept reminding me that it was his sickness and not to take anything personally, he strongly resisted and fought against us when we insisted, him to get help and get treated. And finally, when we got him to start the treatment, he would go back to his old ways after the treatment. My mother kept repeating and repeating to him that he should get the treatment and over the years several attempts were made, but no medical treatment worked on him, and he continued drinking.

There were some rare moments when he would snap out of his drinking spree and come back to us as his true self. He would be the man I remembered in my childhood days; we would talk like we used too. There were many times in his life when he would call me by my name and when I would turn and look at him, I would sense he wanted to tell me something, something important and I could feel that he really wanted to tell me, but he would not say anything. He'd just say it was nothing or he forgot. Sometimes he would call me and ask me to sit beside him while he drank or was having dinner, he would say nothing, but he'd say just stay for a while, while he shared his dinner or lunch with me. Now you see why I hoped if we could go back in time, for moments like this or to even save someone you love. If only I could go back in time, if only. Towards the last few years of his life my relationship with my father was at its worst, I had nothing against him I only loved him, but he did not want me home any longer and asked me not to come back. I knew he didn't mean it; we had the biggest fight of our lives. I wasn't speaking with him for a while, but everything was lost between us after that fight. I was shown the door and I never spoke nor seen him after that. The next occasion I saw him was for his funeral.

I never seen anyone drink that much and I saw a different kind of look in his eyes, it was like alcohol had become water for him an elixir. He was at edge, restless and couldn't contain himself as he began drinking, I saw his greed for the liquid, like it was his absolute necessity, a true hungry vampirish behavior seeking blood he drank and drank for days together, and it didn't seem like he was going to stop. I knew I had to do something, and I did what was required and it wasn't an easy job, nor a pleasant sight to watch, it was difficult to extends I cannot begin to explain. Those events drew us apart even more and he made it clear he wanted me gone out of his life for good. That was the last time he spoke to me or I to him, I left home without saying anything to him. Honestly from his face I could really tell he had enough of me, and I saw that he no longer wanted me there ever. I just didn't know what to say, this wasn't a game for me, there was clearly nothing to win here but lose, and the spite and wrath in my father's face said it all, he wanted to hurt me, but he was letting me go.

The day I got a call of his death, I was relieved, not because he died but finally, I thought he was at peace, finally he could rest and stay still. I truly believed he was in a better place, suddenly everything about him was no longer in the present. No more new memories will be created with him anymore struck me hard and just like that everything about him became just memories and all I could think about him were good ones. I wished I could teleport back in time to be with him in the last few moments of his life so I could tell him everything I wished to say to him. I didn't want to leave things as they were, I wanted to make amends and repair our relationship which was broken and had lost its direction. I wanted to let him know that he was and will always be my hero, my superman who carried me around in his arms when I was a kid. Who build strength in me by being stern, who educated me when I was ignorant and who loved me in ways, I wasn't aware off?

While I sat next to his body, just me and him, I could already feel that he was in a good place as my mind was in peace. I told him everything I had to tell him, I thanked him for all he gave me starting from this amazing life. There are only things for me to do now, as his son I had a responsibility not just by blood but from emotional and spirituals levels to show the world that he was among the greats that lived. My mind began flooding with memories that seemed forgotten, I was astonished by how it came to me, I remembered moments of my life which seemed forgotten and lost. They were all happy memories, maybe this is how he wanted me to remember him. Instead of feeling an immense sense of loss I felt my soul strengthen by his death, it felt like he left by blessing me with all his strength and his wisdom. I always feel his presence around me, I don't miss him as he is with me, he protects me, and he pushes me to be my best.

There was only once in his life he looked at me and said, "I'm proud of you son." That moment kept replaying on my mind for days. Something shifted inside me I wasn't a boy anymore, I wasn't just a man, I became him, his dreams and wishes were what I wanted to achieve, I became a force with a purpose. I remembered everything he shared with me over the years, how he wanted his family to live, that became my mission, his dreams where big and some scared me, but it was time to do what he wanted, it was time he got to rest in peace and be proud of his family knowing we all loved him for the man he was.

My father always told us, that when he dies, he would he sitting in the clouds high in the sky with beautiful angels in bikinis drinking whisky. Every time we miss him, he said, "Look to the skies and among the stars I will be there with you fighting your fights, consoling you off your sorrows and protecting you from all the bad that tries to hurt you." And this I truly felt. My mother always spoke very highly of him, even after his death our mother always reminded us of who our father truly was. Sometimes great people who failed to reach their greatest potential still die as great men. Maybe they wouldn't get the recognition same as that of a successful man when they are alive but death changes that for these kinds of people, the ones he touched and moved deeply always talk about him with a great level of reverence and love.

Life is strange, we take everything for granted and do not show the gratitude nor the respect for the people and things we have. We expect things to always play by our rules, and think we would have our way, until life hits you hard and reminds you, your nothing but a mortal man living a mortal life, anything might be given to you in abundant quantities, but it can also be taken away from you without warning. Just when you were riding life's waves taking you to the highest highs you could also end up the next moment falling hard and flat on your face experiencing the lowest of lows. This is how life truly is and you got to teach yourself to see both situations in equal measure. So, when you are at your highest highs you ground yourself and be humble and not get carried away and then when you are your lowest you learn to accept your failures with grace and grow from it.

So, if your one of them folks who are in a bad relationship with a loved one, I suggest you swallow your pride and irrespective of the other party's reaction make amends, be relentless in your efforts to making amendments because once they are gone, you have no other choice than live with that pain wondering, what if, things were different. Once they are gone, they are truly gone.

The house became annoyingly silent, otherwise it would have been filled up by his yells, "Why isn't the newspapers in their position, why isn't the lights off? Why is the toilet seat down?" No more of all that, just silence. There was nobody asking me to turn off the TV. Just silence, my mother sitting next to me along with my sister and all of us wondering what life is going to be like moving forward, quietly in that silence. And just like that the winter of our lives were over, the snow that collected all over the years began to melt. Healing set in and the light shined it's light on us.

# Chapter 10
# Dark Night of the Soul

I no longer have any idea who I am, who I was and what I am becoming. Though I walk and interact with hundreds of people in a day I felt lifeless. I felt nothing apart from anger, confusion, and disagreement with the person I have become. I was craving for the light, some sort of warmth because I felt cold, lost, and disappointed. I had lost all meaning in life drifting where the wind took me. I have lost count of the years I have been in this state and now I was getting tired of this purposeless life. Everything about me was becoming foul and rotten, I was falling apart, and my body too was turning against me. I was tired so tired if I fell asleep, I knew I'd never wake up. I was that magnificent ship that set sail to find the promise land and build a life that would thrive, full of abundance. But somewhere in that journey I lost direction, I was lost and now I have been going in circles for a while. Having been out so long, out in sea a terrible madness began to set in me.

I did find land from time to time, but the lands seemed cursed with lifelessness, the air was foul, and it smelt like death, the sun was hidden, and it seemed like night wherever I went. Fear deeply rooted, fear consumed me, the sailors all in conflict, frustrated and angry feeling deceived from the promise of riches that they would receive once they reached promise land, instead here they were lost in sea and losing faith on the captain who hid in his room. My whole life was turned upside down, and inside outside, exposing my vulnerable side, for anyone to take advantage off. The plan was to find this promise land and turn my life around but deeper and deeper we sailed more and more horrors unfolded.

It felt like the old me was dying and falling out of existence and there was nobody now to run the show. The new me was in there somewhere he was just taking shape and form. Felt like I was in several depressions, the mind kept questioning everything and my emotions were running the show all by themselves, my insides were in complete chaos. I kept repeating self-destructive patterns even when I knew I shouldn't be doing them. There was nothing I could do to stop myself either. I would think, no, I'm not going to do it and then without much of a big fight or resistance I would end up doing it. I was in debt with every credit card maxed out, spending months repaying the debts and then when I am just making it back, I would go back into my self-destructive patterns and amass more debt. Felt like a very immature kid, throwing tantrums all the time wanting candy. Even when I knew candy was bad for health and I needed to find balance. Every time I came with a plan, and I would focus all my strength to make a recovery just in a couple of days I would act out of control and destroy any progress I had made for weeks. Nothing seemed good enough for me and I aimed for loft sky-high dreams. Not that my dreams where unachievable but nothing in me co-operated.

I would make plans and break them at the speed I made them. I ended every month with no money and when the salary came the cycle would repeat. It was more than exhausting; I could not stop myself from repeating these acts felt like I was punishing myself and I wondered why I would treat myself like this. I always felt like I lacked everything, was it money, health, or happiness. It was a trap, getting out of it seemed impossible an unsolvable puzzle. Felt like I reached a new and improved rock bottom I couldn't get out of. It didn't seem like I really wanted to find the promised land and I have started the journey defeated and was looking forward to only defeat. I was rebelling with every part of myself, and my emotions were in a complete state of anarchy. I spent money I haven't earned yet on alcohol and women, thanks to credit cards for making it possible. Every time I tried to reason with myself and tried talking myself out of my destructive ways, I would slide right in deeper.

What was the meaning of all this? I wondered, what am I trying to prove to myself by doing all this? The only person I was hurting was me. But due to the lack of patience to get to where I wanted and with the need to control everything, I destroyed everything. I have lost all fear of destroying myself and felt maybe this is the way. But deep, deep down still somewhere inside of me I knew what I wanted, which was to turn my life around to an extend that I bring prosperity, peace, an abundance of wealth and happiness for my family. But no matter what or how hard I tried I just seemed to fail at it so miserably and easily. In the early stages, I would resist and retaliate with such devotion and strength but then I would fall with equal intensity. I worked hard, as hard as one could ever imagine, but no, I reaped no benefit from it. I just felt robbed and used instead, nothing I did felt inspired or easy, it felt burdening that it wasn't easy to bear, the work was hard and laborious, but I kept at it. Maybe this was the way I reasoned, maybe this is how I get there I convinced myself, but no, when no reward came, I drank more and more. And when it got to the time to stop I couldn't, I acted out of habit that I built over the years. What worried me most was I was running out of ideas that would help my situation, and I felt drained and very tired, you might imagine I was thin and weary no it was the opposite I was so overweight my knees and angles couldn't bear the weight. I was so out of shape I couldn't recognize myself. I no longer had the slightest hint who I was staring at in the mirror.

Then a few souls came into my life and added fuel to that fire, those names will not be mentioned as they aren't even worth the mention. Greedy, selfish souls who tortured me more which send me spiraling out of control, all they contributed was madness to my already maddening mind, they introduced more chaos to my already chaotic life. They twisted and turned my buttons in ways that amused them, while I carried the burden of all their work. They came in the disguise of heavenly beings with godly gifts promising great rewards while they emotionally, physically drained me of all what was left of me. Nothing felt holy nor divine about them, they were individuals deeply rooted in greed, jealously, selfishness, insecurities that I have never experienced before, the more they claimed to be noble and divine the more vial and demon like they behaved. Emotional vampires they were walking in suits claiming to be Gods among us common men.

I started to lose sleep at night, and I'd wake up with panic attacks, I smoke cigarette after cigarette to calm my mind.

Even the friends I made then would be plotting against me, trying to fill their own bellies, nothing seemed to satisfy them than to use me for their gains and then humiliate me. I wanted to run away as far as I could, but no, I wasn't a coward and no matter what, I decided I would survive this darkness. Nothing seemed to be under my control, I felt like a puppet being taken for a ride, which wasn't pleasant even one bit. Every vulnerable part of me was brought to light and examined and judged. Felt like I was just a spare part waiting to be replaced, now the fight was from within, I had to take a leap of faith or perish completely before their eyes. These people came into my life in the form of my bosses, colleagues and friends. Suddenly, the whole attention was turned away from me to them as they were taking me on a ride of deceit. I couldn't understand anything that happened at those times, it felt deliberate and purposeful most of the time, like a victim being hunted I had to keep running. Wonder what the universe was trying to communicate to me by sending all these people into my life. My surrounding was exactly the way I felt within, they were a perfect reflection and I felt like I had no power over it even when I knew I could control the way I felt. If sucking up to them and kissing their ass was what was needed to be given, to get the credit and achieve the success I deserved, then I wanted no part of it. *If kissing their assess and hailing them as Gods is what they wanted, then I wasn't going to give them that satisfaction, I'll just do my job as best as I could no matter how difficult they tried to make it for me,* I thought. I'll just come and give my best that's all I could do, while they called out my incompetence, I only saw more of theirs, I slowly stopped paying attention to them as much as they tried to break me apart. And started to bring the focus back to me.

This was a time in my life I took the wrong turn, feeling like I made the right choice but walked into hell fire instead. I was tested, judged, and disrespected by imbeciles in my opinion when I think of it now. But if it weren't for destiny to happen like that then I wouldn't have reached here today. While I was undergoing the most painful trials of my life, I always carried around a philosophy that the universe had the best interest for me, and it wouldn't put me through any of these trials until it was required. I persevered as much as I could, I fought through it even when I was exhausted and weak, I always knew I wasn't perfect and that many things in me required change. I was already a self-critical person criticizing myself so I'd improve and find this promise land hidden deep inside me so I could change my life for the best.

My aim was to become the best version of myself, so I'd be able to handle any situation thrown at me. I wanted to win under any circumstances and hence start this journey of transformation into this perfect version that was craving to see the light. So, one day when I succeed, I'd have the power to change many lives for the best. This is my sole intent and my soul purpose, I wanted to experience success in every aspect of my life to any level I wanted. But I wanted to achieve all this in the right way, through the right path laid for me, which I was searching for, I wanted to do it in a level of dignity and respect without having to kiss anybody's ass or deceive anybody to become successful. I wanted to be the light to souls drowning in sorrows and rescue them from their own self-defeating ways. An example that they could look upon to, to turn around their own lives. I wanted to be the man who could inspire anyone to dare to run after their dreams. But there I was trapped, still searching, and hoping. A misfit that never belonged anywhere, with no place to call of his own, with debts which he was creating, a person with the abilities to succeed but having trouble choosing this path, having no clue what it is he should be doing, drifting through the space and time aimless falling and failing to live up to his own dreams, sabotaging everything along the way getting nowhere and being a complete nobody.

I was a stranger to my own self, and I had no clue how to solve this riddle of what I was turning out to be. Every time something good came into my life I would panic and sabotage it. I would immediately dismiss it saying it's not what I wanted or how I wanted to succeed. I no longer knew if I even wanted to get to where I wanted. My sabotaging patterns haunted me and discouraged me because I was tired living these demeaning patterns, I wanted to get out of this so badly every cell in my body ached for a change. Any normal individual who would have been paying attention to the signs, would have successfully turned his life around by now. But I was rebelling with my own self, caught between the outer world and my emotions I could no longer keep up with both.

How much did I really know about myself? I felt like I have abandoned my own self, I could not hear the quiet voice in my mind who was trying to guide me anymore, instead I did exactly the opposite of what it wanted for all these years and now it's gone. I wasn't owning my failures and being okay with it, I had to stop torturing myself for things that happened in my past, I had to move on and heal. I had to forget my failures and look forward to the better parts of life that was waiting for me. I had to take the journey within, to know my own self and set myself free, this was the only solution. To honor the soul in me was the way, I knew this was the way, and the only way forward and firstly I needed to get out of my own way to make these changes. I had to learn to help my own self for the better good. I had to learn to rediscover the wonders in me that I rejected. I had to start the journey into myself to truly bring the changes I wished to see and feel in me, and the same experiences I wished for in the outer world. Only when you change from within can the circumstances in your outer experience change.

Slowly and eventually, I started this journey, but this time I did it for myself. I wanted to live this life for me for a change, and I stopped thinking about what the world would think or how people would judge me. It wasn't easy cause I had to redo all the work that I have done all these years. And this was discouraging. I wondered if my father too went through all these trials, I wondered if this was the reason for him to give up. I could imagine it being the reason because only I knew the amount of work and effort that needed to be re-done in terms of personal growth and the changes to be made within me and also going after the things that mattered to me in the physical world no matter how scary it felt, and I did do it all and there wasn't anyone to witness it, only I knew the different remedies I tried, the late night's I stayed up working or studying or reading trying to find the solution to the problems in my life or to pass an exam, to meet office deadlines and make plans to do the things necessary for my dreams. I know that people were around to only see the worst parts of me and write me off. I could feel, how much pain he should have been in and then suddenly discovering that he's got to do all what he's done all over again, it's exhausting might as well give up, right?

For me, if I could pull this through and somehow make it meant a win for my father as well. This was worth giving a shot. But when it comes to, executing in the real world nothing goes according to plan, right? Well, I used my experience with failure to help me through those times. I have experienced so much failure at this point it did not bother me anymore. I was alright with failure, and it didn't bother me, and my focus shifted to be consistent on my efforts, to just act, by acting in the right direction without having any expectation of the outcome. I had to give myself the time and the credit for taking the effort without rewarding myself with alcohol or other forms of debauchery. This was the tricky bit, but it had to be done.

Having depended religiously on weed, mushrooms, alcohol, and a constant need to escape on adventures whenever it got emotionally overbearing it was impossible for me to change immediately. My need to indulge in any substance was to escape what I was feeling. I'd do anything to escape my emotions and go to any extend to get me the kind of fix that I required for that moment. This gave me a false sense of satisfaction making me think that I am doing something with my life as it made me feel alive, so letting go of the addiction was challenging. Living the sober life was an impossible thought at first, because I had to do what I wanted when it came to de-stressing from work which was doing things I shouldn't be doing as it was the only way I knew to relax. Using the drugs to de-stress did not work in the long run as I kept avoiding my emotions and I kept running into the same problems. So, then I quit weed and mushrooms completely and allowed myself to drink, I always found a reason to justify my mind I needed that alcohol or the shrooms or the weed or the booty call or something as I couldn't be happy without it, giving up everything was not possible. Finally, I got my problems down to just alcohol, the thought of being sober was too dreadful because the root cause for needing alcohol or drugs was that I wasn't happy, and there was no other way I knew happiness but through them.

No matter how many attempts I made and no matter how well I did in other areas of my life due to my need to drink and sex a stranger up made several problems in my life. It emotionally arrested me from truly making a complete recovery. I knew I had to give up everything that made me feel low or reminded me of my old self. If I had to do this, I had either completely shut myself in a room or learn to control my urges. Mentally and emotionally, it was possible, partly because I really needed to change. But I failed to keep it up and would relapse and when I did, I would completely fall over to the dark side and even before I could control myself, I would have done the damage against all the progress I have made. Now this cycle happened for months, and months became years. Yes, it took years, and I did it anyway, each time getting better, inch by inch I reclaimed myself. It was painfully difficult it wasn't easy at any level, but I was relentless I have decided no matter how much time it takes and no matter how many times I fail someday I would make it.

Out of a thousand jobs I applied I would maybe get three calls back and I would end up getting rejected in all the interviews, but it was okay, cause every time I felt like I almost lost it all and there was no hope, the universe would come in and help me out and I kept afloat. I read and watched many videos of the many gurus out there in the modern world. I tried all kinds of strategies and methods and when nothing worked, I depended on my own instincts and intuition. When I failed to listen to my instinct and intuition, I would go back to the guru's, you name them I would have either read something they wrote or watched a video of him. I kept at it day in and day out, always looking ahead with hope always fighting back when I lost my way. Motivating myself, paying attention to myself and learning to accept and love myself for what I was and not giving a care in the world for the nay Sayers.

It did not move fast, sometimes it felt like it barely moved, most times it felt like I slipped back to my old ways, but I got back up always. I did not let anyone know what I was going through, I had to do this by myself, I had to do this for my father and myself and I knew I will succeed, it was just a matter of time. But time worked extremely slow for me, and I couldn't show any form of success physically but within me I knew where I was heading, and I choose to believe only in myself and no matter what or how the world judged me. Brick by brick I reconstructed myself, and if the foundation was weak and part of the wall fell, I got back up to rebuild myself better and stronger. Everything requires its times; it wasn't easy turning over the leaf and expecting miracles to fall out every second or every now and then. The process was painfully slow, I would try and keep things up for days but the heaviness in my heart never seemed to change. *Maybe I needed more time,* I thought, or maybe it wasn't meant to be, there were self-doubts, but I chose to believe in myself for the first time in my life. I always remember this part of the journey when I started my attempts towards my recovery, and I always knew if I kept this up, I would achieve the change I was looking for. But things didn't come to me easily.

I remember no matter how hard I tried and no matter how long I could keep myself sober no miraculous break through happened nor did anything small and encouraging happen with ease. Every day seemed like another day of struggle and another day felt like any other days of the same struggle, I would break, out of boredom of this routine, I would get so frustrated to have always put in so much effort, but it wouldn't get me anywhere, the more I tried the more the outer world came crashing on me. The process was exhausting and just tedious, disciplined, and laborious. Why wasn't I feeling good about myself? I wondered, am I not doing this right? I started developing several other problems like lack of sleep and excessive weight. I was still drowning in a hopelessness I couldn't explain. I kept at it and tried to not think about the negative thoughts that sprouted in my mind, but I wasn't making any progress, it felt like I was stuck in quicksand and any movement only lodged me deeper into the pit.

I could feel how misaligned I was with myself, and I was exhausted and every part of me wished for a break. Felt like no matter which direction I went I ended up at the same place, I was lost, and I no longer had a clue to what I should be doing. Despite all this, when I am still stuck in these moments, I would do what was right intellectually even when intuitively I was completely out of sync. I felt God, had put an end to the story of my life and wanted me to ever roam in a limbo. Maybe I was cursed like my father and all his brothers and cousins who were victims of this terrible thirst for alcohol. When can I find a solution, what can I do? I had been through quiet a lot and I felt like maybe it was time to give up, throw in the towel and surrender to the mercy of whoever is sitting in the heavens.

At the end we are just chemical reactions happening within ourselves, some of us are a good chemical composure attracting wonderful things into their life, but I feel there are a few of us who are lost souls, cursed souls, trying to find their way back in their lives. Souls that know they don't fit in anywhere, tired of fighting, tired of being taken advantage of, don't complain much, accepts the consequences, always gets blamed for things even when it's never their fault. I know there are some of you who feel this way, we recognize each other while be cross each other on the streets and I see the burden you carry inside yourself hoping someday someone will come and place a hand on your back to say, "You're okay son, you're doing fine."

I know you feel misunderstood most of the time and you don't relate to the masses, I know you don't relate to the ways of the elite and the ass kissers who follow them around. I know you are tired of moving, adjusting, and keeping quiet cause you know you're going to sound like a mad person, I know you stand alone, always judged, and I know you don't need anybody but at least once in a while I know it would be great to have someone that can completely relate with your ideas and views on life rather than living blind following the masses and living a life like most people do, which isn't wrong in anyway but for some unexplainable reason you just can't be like them cause the illusion they are in is not at all enjoyable for you as it is for them, I know you wish to find a place where there are people who you can call your own, a place that feels like home. I know you feel lost and confused while people mock your ideas, mock your ways, and discourage your dreams, while all this time you where there for them and finally when they were saved you fell behind and felt abandoned.

So, we just drift through life hoping that we overcome and conquer these trials and tests thrown upon us, hoping that we are not crazy for being honest and vulnerable and not being like the rest, always looking out for the light, always searching for a place called home that seems lost and hard to find. In the end, all we want is after going through all these tests and trials in life, is to find meaning and peace. I just wanted peace more than anything, and in order to be at peace I had to get away from all the noise. I couldn't be around people, that would make me feel drained and weak. Everything that I feared, grew stronger and stronger in me, I would be facing difficult circumstances and situations repeatedly. I Always felt like people grouped against me and they had malicious intentions against me. I just couldn't be around the group of people I was around then, they felt toxic. Everything seemed strange and unfamiliar like everything was planned to make me feel depressed and defeated. I couldn't tell if I was sleeping or if I was awake, I couldn't tell reality from illusion. It felt like I was living my nightmares all at once and it was taking a toll on me, I wished for it to end, but I had a promise to keep and there was no turning back from it.

My anxiety levels were high at these times, so I smoked a lot of joints to relax. I remember one night sitting on the beach all by myself staring at the full moon's reflection on the water I lit a joint and smoked it while chewing on some magic shrooms. I felt a sudden soothing cold wind blow through my chest and suddenly I was sucked into the water, and I was sinking deeper and deeper towards the seabed. While I was sinking, I could clearly see the moon and it was huge, white round ball. While this was happening, a beautiful song was playing in the background, I saw the bubbles escape from my mouth to the surface and the reflection of the moon on the surface flutter like a flag blowing in the wind. I was extremely calm and happy, I was at peace, I was free no longer trapped by the emotions in my body, no longer trapped by the thoughts in my mind and no longer trapped by the rules of man, I was free in a way I felt no other man was.

The music came from the water, and it massaged my aura, and I became one with everything. The next day I woke up on the beach feeling the same way I felt during my trip, I felt wonderful and fantastic. Though the world outside seemed the same something shifted in me that night and I felt different, and I left feeling like magic. I was awakened, like I returned to my body after centuries. My life started taking a turn for the better. I wasn't exactly out of the dark, but I wasn't afraid of it anymore, I became one with it, I accepted it, and slowly and gradually I began taking back the power I gave away. Like a newborn baby I started making my way back to life. If you are reading this book, I would like to tell you that hope is never lost to the man or woman who truly wants a better life. It's okay to be scared and it's okay to be vulnerable, do not take things seriously while you are down and lying in the gutter. Cut yourself some slack, give yourself a break, pat yourself on your back, get back up on your feet and fight the good fight ahead of you. If you're alone don't be afraid only the strongest get the toughest fights. Don't pay attention to the world that is hurting you, mocking you and doing their best to rip you off your confidence. Don't waste a second trying to teach them a lesson, you're just going to waste time and energy, instead follow your heart listen to your soul and do the right thing, and you will be fine.

# Chapter 11
# The Calm After the Storm

The time was around 6:00 am on a Saturday morning, the sun was out, and some of its rays was blocked by the leaves on a tree and the light that managed to escape the leaves made its impact on a windowsill by the tree, the light refracted through the glass and lit the room from the night's darkness. A couple of hummingbirds flew around near the windowsill dipping their beaks in the flowers on the tree. Strong smell of black coffee filled the air, my eyes opened to the sight of humming birds flying about from flower to flower and a beautiful brown eyed woman handed me a mug of coffee, she got dressed, wrote me a note and stuck it on my fridge, she turned one last time and I looked at her sitting on my bed sipping coffee, as the sun light fell on her, like a spot light cast from the heavens so I'd get one good look at her before she smiled picked up her bag and left my newly rented apartment. That was Juliana my neighbor, she broke up with her boyfriend a couple of months back and we got to talking in the corridor, some consoling was done, might have watched a movie, and had dinner and then one thing led to another guess you could figure out the rest.

I drank my coffee and felt like a brand-new person in my brand-new rented apartment, I got out of bed opened the window and a brand-new day waited for me. *I wonder what adventure life had for me today,* I thought, *I wondered what surprise stay hidden.* I read the note on the fridge which read, "Call me," and she left her number. It's been months since I've watched her on her balcony doing her yoga, who knew we'd end up doing the downward facing dog together. I got into my beach shorts, planned for the beach this weekend. The day looked great for a beach day, the space around me felt so different. It was bright and it felt light, and the warm air was intimately hugging me, blowing my shirt gently to the side. The warmth of the morning sun warmed my skin and formed a layer of heat over my skin. The elevator door slides open and smiling faces looked back at me and a smile cracked across my face. Warm greetings escaped our lips, and more happy people got into the elevator. There were young kids excited as their parents planned to take them out for the day, their excitement spread like a disease and a childlike excitement build in me as well now I was really looking forward to having a fun relaxing day at the beach.

The car started I was set to go; the radio was playing love songs. As I pulled out of the car park, I was stopped by the guy who owned a food stand outside my apartment on the main road. I bought fresh baked croissants and drove off towards the beach, the car smelled of delicious croissants and the music from the radio was so calm and soothing, I wondered if all this was real or if I was tripping. I have never experienced life so beautifully without being high. I was feeling warm, happy, and satisfied like I never was before. I felt light as a feather floating through the air. I was held in traffic by the traffic signal, but nothing seemed to bother me. I was in a peaceful trance and connected to the flow of life, I wasn't in a hurry I had all the time in the world.

I planned to walk the bridge that leads to the beach. I really wished I had the words to explain how awesome the sight was. Water on either side, the water reflecting the perfect sky blue, boats cruising by and jet skis speeding past under the bridge. I walked towards the beach eating the croissants listening to music through my earphones. A Labrador on the back of a jeep with its roof retracted was barking at a kid on her father's shoulder, she had her right hand extended holding a cookie pointing it towards the Labrador. An angry business was stuck in the traffic behind the jeep, he was in convertible too, yelling at the top of his voice while his wife looked away from him with a fed-up look. Pop corns, I smell pop corns, the smell was coming from the direction of the beach, the wind carried the smell further back and the kid on her father shoulders shouted popcorn with a smile on her face.

Guess I made the right decision to walk or else I would have been stuck in traffic. Three boys jetted passed me in skateboards, a tourist was asking for directions near the junction and a sea of people were pouring in from all directions to the junction, all heading to the beach. A group of kids were talking about a superhero movie they wanted to watch after their swim, young lovers were kissing while waiting for their ice cream. Cotton candy vendor calling out the kids for cotton candy. A group of super models like looking girls in their swimsuits were taking pictures near the surfboard rental shops. Yes, all the men turned back as they crossed them to get a good look at their asses. The queue for the giant wheel was growing into the line where people were waiting to get their morning coffee from a coffee shop. There was rows and rows of shops, with fun games for kids, all kinds of gifts, souvenir shops. I was making my way to the men's changing room. A small boy stood at the entrance of the changing room crying while his dad shouted out from the showers to his son, "Hold on, I'm coming." I got myself a locker, kept my bag, phone, and sunglasses in them and then I headed to the beach. There is something you didn't know about me I was born for the waters I loved to swim; I think I was a merman in my past life. I made my way to the beach, found the perfect spot to place my towel, ran towards to the water until I was waste deep in the water and then I dived into the blue.

With my goggles on I could see everything clear through the blue and I swan deeper and deeper into sea, taking random dives to the seabed, collecting seashells and corals a hobby of mine. I swam away from the crowd towards the reefs as I dove in, to my surprise, I saw hundreds of star fish lying on the seabed, sea horses swimming in between the corals and lionfishes, clown fishes swimming by, felt like I died and went to paradise. I would float on the surface when I came up for air, lying on my back looking up into the blue skies, drifting through the water with my ears submerged, I would hear noises of jet skis from under the water, feeling the warmth of the sun hit my body, drifting randomly listening to sounds through the water with my eyes closed, lying on the water felt like I was on a waterbed feeling the waves taking my body up and down as the water flowed by me. I was completely relaxed and free, I felt so alive that I did not want to leave. After swimming for a couple of hours I lay on the beach letting the sun dry my body, fell asleep for an hour woke up when I realized I was being covered in sand by two naughty kids who were laughing when I looked at them. I was completely covered from my neck down.

I got off the beach having sand all over my body, everyone was looking at me smiling and some women laughing while I got out of the sand. I chased the kids shouting pretending I was about to catch them; they ran in two different directions laughing their lungs out. I managed to catch hold of one kid, and I put him on my shoulder as I headed to the water and playfully threw him in the water. He jumped back up splashing water on me and then the other rascal too joined him. Laughing along with them I splashed water back at them After a while I waved them goodbye as I headed to the showers. Had the best shower of my life, I felt refreshed and smelled like the ocean. I walked into a nearby restaurant located on the beach, ordered a chicken club sandwich and a back coffee. I was sitting facing the sun and the sea, people were lying on the beach warming up to the sun some for a tan before the sun set. Lovers walked by holding hands, sandcastles were being built and some were being demolished. I sat there enjoying the view taking it all in like a drink or a snack while I sipped on my coffee and ate my club sandwich. I felt like a whole other person living a completely different life.

I paid the bill and watched the sun set to a glorious day. I felt light like I was weightless or in space away from the earth's gravity floating freely through the cosmos. Music was playing in my ears through my earphones I was trying to find the song which played on the radio that morning. As I neared the bridge, and night was falling upon us and the streetlights came on, and other lights on shops buildings lit up the night.

The place looked even more stunning at night. I walked back to the car with a smile on my face hoping the day would never end. While I was crossing the bridge, I saw a man carrying a transparent plastic bag with four goldfishes in it. I have been saving up to buy a pup, but it cost too much, and it is a bigger responsibility, maybe I should start small and buy a fish instead I thought. Got to my car and started driving home thinking of buying the fish the next day.

You must be wondering if I am high, but no, dead sober, sorry to disappoint you and believe me if you can. It's been 11 months now and I'm going strong, some days are easy, I get by them well and I feel good, some days are okay, but I must put in a little effort. But there are those days when it gets very hard and I almost go overboard, on a very honest level I really don't want to go overboard and so I somehow keep afloat. Oh, no I didn't turn this ship around that easy, there was like a million attempts at least. Sometimes I would cruise through days and by mistake, seriously by pure fucking accident I would drive to a pub and think I could handle just one drink, but no, I would break. Like I said a million attempts later I found the rhythm. Guess I was fed up being stuck without any growth, I wanted to be freer and feel more alive. I just couldn't live anymore and be happy by doing drugs and alcohol, there was more to me, and I wanted to experience and be more. Do not ask me if I miss it, in my opinion it's a very stupid question, yes of course I miss doing the drugs but like I said I am much more than that and when I came to realize that it became easier for me to transition. Nowadays I'm more interested to solve the mysteries of the universe. The clues it has laid in humans, on the planets and throughout the cosmos. I started wondering what if, I could still be me and learn to wield the energy in me to create something awesome, amazing things wouldn't that be cool. If I am part of this universe made of the stuff the universe is made of then maybe I should tune into it and explode with ideas to create rather than destroy. A new addiction grew in me it was to decode the mysteries of the universe, I wanted nothing apart but to be a part of it and express its version of life that it manifested in my body. I no longer could see the person I was before he was just a personality that was developed over time conditioned and sculpted as society wanted.

I am no longer that person, I don't feel like that person, I never was that person, I am just an expression of life created by a cosmic force I'm yet to understand. New urges grew in I wanted to travel to all corners of the planet and not miss a place. I wanted to meet souls across the globe, mingle with them and be one with them. It sucks though the modern age of man is built on many walls in the form of boundaries which separates us as this nationality and this religion or this race and old age concepts like passports, visas, money, tourists, and so on. How long will you be staying? What is the purpose of your visit? Bank statements? And a thousand other questions which I don't get why its required. Guess no matter how intelligent we have become and advanced our technology is we have forgotten to be humane and in order to protect ourselves from our own selves, we have made these rules and divisions and classifications and requirements, what happened to us?

We should be able to move freely, without any requirement but guess learning small things like sharing is forgotten and life is just about money and profiting I guess for the lives of modern man. Well, I had enough, I would dial down the modernity in certain aspects and roam the earths like our ancestors did thousands and thousands of years ago freely. But what to do I need to do what's required at our time, to be able to explore life like I wish it to be. What I meant was I needed money for the travel and hence I had to work. So, I no longer saw my job as a curse but a key to make the business owner richer so he pays me more so I can run after the things that really matter to be. Maybe each age of man over the centuries had its own challenges to live on planet earth at their time. But now when we have reached the age which is in the cusp of many breakthroughs, and there will a million more things we will invent or discover, let us change one thing along with that, lets breaks these walls down, lets cross these boundaries without fear, lets learn to accept and coexist together peacefully. Let's all gather after work, let the DJ play his music, let's all dance around a giant bon fire and lets all make love under the sky, share everything we have and become drunk on life, all free to live and thriving with life.

Sometimes, I felt a constant need to keep moving and I don't understand why? In a state of complete restlessness unable to stay calm and hold the mind still. I am still searching for something and I'm sure it's not out there now, whatever I am looking for is in me. But this urge to keep moving tricks the mind and old habits push me to look for it outside and I'm still learning that all the answers are in me. I am learning to pick up the pieces now and learning to mend it together, I'm learning to put the pieces together and meet the real me. It's kind of exciting and scary the same time as I try to unveil the illusion created by old conditioning and see the true meaning of life and its purest form of expression. It lies deep in me as an emotion and wishes to experience life through my senses and intellectually understand what all this is about and also play a part in it.

Now I sound like I'm high but still no, but the restless in me gets unbearable sometimes, so much energy trying to express itself but not knowing yet in what form it should express itself. This was how I always felt, and these were the times I went so deep into my self-destructive patterns, I just had to spend the energy. Nowadays, I just don't allow myself to go through those destructive ways, I just hold it still and wait for ideas to pop in my mind to express it in creative ways. I keep losing track of time between activities while I sink in deep into thought. For instance, now I am still driving back to my apartment and wondering when I will stop thinking so I can return to the physical world and think of what I need to cook tonight cause the universe is not going to cook that meal for me. Despite having the club sandwich, I was still feeling famished, yes that's what swimming generally does but hunger after swimming in the sea creates a very different kind of hungry. It's the kind of hungry you would relate to a hungry lion chasing a deer or will the beast, like you watch on the discovery channel. The hunger is visibly seen in the lions' eyes otherwise who in their right state of mind even a lion for that matter run after a deer. I mean the deer is very fast, so unless you're hungry to the point you'd kill you cannot chase a deer down right. That's the kind of hunger I relate to after swimming in the sea, at this point I'd run after a deer if I had too, you know if I was one among them sexy cats running wild in the jungle. But I either had to cook or order in.

Having had a great, fun day and excited I'd be out the next day shopping for my fish. I decided to treat myself to some Chinese. Rebuilding yourself is one of the hardest things you can do in your life, especially when you are plagued with self-doubt and fear. But there is nothing more empowering once you start that journey. Re-building you, is a doorway to explore yourself much better than you ever had before. Do you really know yourself? We are so absorbed into the outer experience of life we end up doing things what we think we want and most of the time it ends up in a disappointment or you're not entirely satisfied, and you continue this search for fulfillment by desiring things on your physical reality not paying any attention to that inner voice. We end up running after things which seems like it's going to fulfill us but when it doesn't, we keep looking for it again in the outside world. We end up knowing and understanding everybody around us and yet we wake up at the end of our lives not having a clue who we truly are.

I guess there is no perfect way to live, the whole thing is just an experience, but whose experience you are living is the real question. Is it really your experience or is it a programmed experience which you are not even aware of? Have you ever felt like your separate from your body, the name given to you, the labels you have, son, daughter, husband, wife, brother, sister and so on? Have you ever felt that you are beyond your name or your labels and all this pretend to be this person as others see you and you fulfilling the various roles labelled by them is just an act or a program you react to, while the real you is somewhere in your body dying to come out and reveal itself? Yes, to live in this world we must play various roles but are you doing it the way people want it or from the ego, or are you doing it in your way, the way your soul wants to experience it. Aren't you tired trying to fit in where you feel like you don't, aren't you tired of waiting for a sign or an external experience to set you free?

It's this wait I feel constantly, I'm waiting for something to happen, and I don't know what it is and I'm relying on this event to happen, so I am happy and fulfilled or set free. But I can't quite figure out why I should wait or why something on the outside should happen for my happiness. Its somehow fed into our psyche that we need to work hard and earn it, for anything, and now even happiness itself is like a distant dream, for me, to work upon to finally deserve it. No matter how much we are educated and how many degrees or money we have, I don't think any of it will matter, if we are not happy. The truth is you want to be happy now, exactly the way you are now, without having to work for it and without the things you feel you need in order to be happy. You deserve to be happy just for being you, don't you?

Nothing was easy for me while learning to quit the substances that controlled my life, as I always had the thought of going out for a drink, the worst situations where when someone invited me or if I was passing by similar roads, or even sub-consciously driving to a pub while hesitating to go back home because I wanted to do more than go back and rest. Some days I would be staring out the window wondering how to kill the time. The boredom was the hardest moments to bare but then I was always happy to have come such a long way. There was a time in my life I couldn't get by without a drink or weed, the very thought without it was an impossible thing to imagine. Somewhere down the line I was somehow convinced that I was meant to do this as nothing else made me happy. Now that I've finally stopped, and I'm glad that I did, but now I'm thinking, now what. What am I supposed to do with my life? Yes, I really wished to take a break just to sit down and breathe but I couldn't even do that because I was completely broke.

It's great when the mind drifts into a daydreaming state, where anything is possible, and everything happens instantaneously but in real life specially after I got sober everything seemed to take so much time. Felt like time slowed down and I felt every second tick and every minute pass me by. During my getting high days I would lose track of time, like literally wake up and wonder what happened in the last couple of hours and missing out the weekend entirely was a thing. I would wake up and wonder what I did and how I lost all this money, and I wouldn't be able to remember it. Once I did the same thing for three consecutive weekends, that was to go to my room, drink until I couldn't stand, while getting high on other stuff, while watching a movie and ordering in and finally passing out and waking up the next morning hurrying for work. I did this for three weekends continuously and on the fourth weekend when I ran out of the booze and drugs and out of money I realized that three weeks have passed by as I thought only one week passed by as I was in a drug hazed loop doing the same things in a particular order making three weeks seem identical making me feel I was reliving the week all over again which tricked me into believing I was in the same week when it all started.

Picking up and rebuilding yourself is an impossible task in the beginning, the first week time went by so slow it felt like years and couple of grey hairs popped on my head. Relapsing gets so easy, as every muscle and cell in your body has it in its memory. Getting out of the head space wherein you think that your addiction is what your meant to be doing in your life as it's the only activity that gives you a sense of happiness and purpose keeps tricking the mind to relapse. I had relapsed a million times at least, but when I went back to the old ways it brought about the old emotions, and the feeling of being stuck and helplessness and wanting to change and experience new things in life would come back again. And then you're in this loop taking that step and falling back, taking that step, and falling back a very vicious torturous cycle. But I was serious about quitting my old ways and wanting to change so I kept pushing forward, I have lost years of my life to be exact 11 years.

Sometimes my mind would be strong, but my body would behave like it needed to go back, sometimes it would be the other way around, something it would be both wanting to go back. The worst scenario is when I would be doing great and I wouldn't be wanting to do it mentally nor will my body be asking for it, but I would just act out of habit and fall into the old ways. I just couldn't understand that behavior at all, couldn't understand it the slightest way, when I would be drinking knowing I should not, and my mind would agree what I am doing is wrong and it's against my will and even my body would have had enough but still I do it, and I wouldn't even stop myself. I act as though I have no control over myself, or I ignore the warning my mind and body signals me, I just don't understand it at all why I would do that to myself. I would have gone like a month without anything and one fine day I'd just drive to a pub and my mind would be trying to stop me, but I won't listen, order a pint and my body would begin to feel sick and I'd go through with it despite all the signals and signs.

This feeling of being out of control was frightening to extends I cannot even imagine explaining but then I also had epic nights where I really enjoyed for that moment and then wake up the next day miserable. I couldn't understand why I behaved like this and how it got to this. I used to be the opposite of what I was but guess I had enough of playing by the rules too, because it got me nowhere and I allowed myself to spiral out of control to this extend.

Nobody is going to help you pick up your pieces, trust me nobody has the time for it, nor do they care to that extend. In my case I had no excuse I already had my father as an example, they would mercilessly blame me anyway, but if you must know I have no regrets, not even one for having done what I had done to myself. Looking back now I don't see myself living any other way than the way it all panned out. I guess eventually I would have put myself through this as I was already exploding within me before it all started. Never have I ever been so connected to my father before, never have I ever understood him better than now, now I understand how difficult it was to get out. I should have been more compassionate; I should have never abandoned him like I did towards the end. But it seemed like there was no other way then because he threw me out of my own house, and I accepted it and left without even putting a fight back and helping him. If I did put up a fight and helped him maybe I wouldn't have been in this situation in the first place. But I guess it was how it was meant to be as I allowed it to happen this way even when I had the power to act differently.

Life is tough in that way it slaps you hard with karma, lessons to be learnt, trust me if your too ignorant to identify them, learn from them, change your course, and grow from your own experiences living would be like getting sucked into quicksand. You would be living in cycles of repetitive thought and action being too stubborn to learn from your mistakes and dying one day as an old man full of regrets. Make as many mistakes as you want but let them be new ones at least. If you're the kind of person whose got your head way up your ass where your ego is, may God save you, because that's the one place even the light can't travel too.

# Chapter 12
# Soul Story

Sitting on my couch and staring at the fish swimming around reminded me of my dark and light sides in me, both telling a story of their own. Both the fish seemed to be peacefully coexisting in my fish tank but the darkness and light within me where in conflict with each other thus producing this duality and the mind constantly struggled with choosing a side. When I tried silencing the darkness it got stronger and wanted to express itself, that side of me wanted to be acknowledged and accepted the way it is. Buying these fish marked the actual start of my recovery it was some sort of sub-conscious trigger wherein I no longer had to fight the thoughts as I began to see past these dual natures in me. Learning to accept my short coming was necessary, making peace and understanding my darkness was the only way forwards. It was the start to learning and understanding myself as a whole and fall in love with this source of life or energy which existed in me and everything around me in this planet and in the universe. It was about finding a balance between the two, I found the habits that rooted of my darkness as trivial, small, immature and a complete misunderstanding of myself as I always felt like I harmed something in me to which

I wasn't paying attention and to whom none of what I was doing mattered to it. They came to life not to destroy me but to awaken me and guide me to the truth that lay deep within myself. The darkness became my friend and guide, the darkness made the light easy to find as now I chose not to identify myself with it but accept it for what it is and paid attention to what it is trying to tell me. Every seeker will find it if he is true to himself and his cause to find it, its within him waiting with open arms irrespective how screwed and twisted you feel about your life or yourself.

It's never too late and it will always receive you with arms wide open even if you feel you're not worthy of it. The light is there to remind you that you are in every sense worthy of anything as you are light, and the darkness is there to guide you to it asking you to understand that you are very much part of the darkness as much as you are of the light. Because without the complete acceptance of the darkness you will not be able to appreciate and accept the light. Though they seem different in nature they are the driving force that leads you to see the bigger picture which is life. Once when you learn to have them peacefully exist within you like my two fish in the fish tank you will understand that they are not separate but one. A blissful sensation of peace filled me, I felt like I've freed myself from the illusions that were controlling me. I felt no fear of anything, I did not fear the things that used to control me and my reason to change and embrace a new path too was not out of fear of the demons that haunted me. It was out of pure fascination and a love to experience the parts of life I was missing; I wanted my life to be a continuous, harmonious experience how the real intelligent source of life in me wanted to live. A life that might make no sense to another but a universal experience for me. A life where I wasn't worried about the wealth, health, fame, or success but live like a being full of life having enriching experiences from my soul.

And if I were to die today, I want to go quietly in the night having beautiful memories of the short time I had here on this planet. A peaceful co-existence with the source of life in me which is at peace with everything in the cosmos. I no longer wanted to be identified by the personality I have derived over the years, they were built purely on survival and influenced by emotions that grew from dark circumstances. I was taught to detach from them and let go off the demons that were weighing me down and to stop resisting the growth I deserved. I thought about the hallucinations I experienced while I visited the shaman and realized whatever I experienced were an expression of my inner mental and emotional state, it is time now to release and forget the ways of the old me and embrace this new path to a new me. I realized I have been holding energies that served no purpose for my current journey I was set to embark, and it was time to move on from my past and to stop living in the illusion that others had some control over me. The destructive behavior I have developed were an unhealthy expression of the emotions, people, and experiences I have suppressed deep within my mind. It was time to make peace, forgive myself for not having done what should have been done at times when I was deep in the clutches of ignorance and a slave of my habits.

I no longer felt the urge to travel back in time to change anything, I guess I wouldn't have done it any other way than how it had happened, I am happy now and I am powerful for

I have awakened from this terrible dream which I thought I would never wake up from. Gratitude filled me, I was high on life in a completely different way, I was released from the burdens I have carried for long and far, I have become one within myself. I could come out of this exile I have put myself through, I am becoming in every way how I want to be, I wished to be with no fear of what people would judge me and with complete acceptance of who I am. It was time to come back to life and live and work for the dreams that were worthwhile and to stop chasing a fantasy to compensate for my losses that hurt my ego, the disappointments that of failure, the pain for all the rejections, the anger that life didn't go my way and the terrible feeling of not being worthy. I could literally see everything clearly once again in my life, I knew exactly what I need to do as this was opposed to what I felt through all these past years. I was blind but now I am making my way to find something that would liberate me, I always thought it would be in the outer world in the form of money, power, success and in the end, it was a powerful change within me, that gave me everything I needed. If you ask me what I have today I'd say nothing, I have accumulated nothing, but I have found my confidence and a true sense of belief in myself and I feel abundant in every way of every dream, every man could dream off.

I am happy just being me, I am happy I survived through my trials even if I suffered and now standing at the crossroads off my life where I stand having lost so much time and having to rebuild my life all over again, I still feel like I have already won. I understood what I was looking for wasn't the money, or the love, success, fame, but to find me, the real me who was trapped under the years of conditioning of the world.

Having to do everything all over again felt like the universe gifting me with a precious second chance, this time I wasn't afraid of winning or losing, I wanted to just live irrespective of the outcome, irrespective of the judgement, I wanted every minute to be exciting full of life an adventurous life like I always wanted to live. No longer will I do mundane tiring work that eats away by soul but rather do work that feed and nourishes my soul, so I thrive and blossom.

For my father who is loved by his family, may he find the peace he always wished, may his soul blossom among the stars in the sky. Like you always said to me, I will look for you among the stars when I miss you. I just wish I'd become half the man you were and hope that anything I accomplish in my life makes you proud, I hope that everything your daughter accomplishes make you proud. I lay my life in tribute to you for if it wasn't for you, I wouldn't be here, I am truly saddened by how our story went but you will live through me always and you will win through my life, every battle that I will have to fight will be for us and your dream you shared with me for our family will be done. I understand completely the battle you had with addiction, I have felt your pain and your struggles, I felt your loss and the feeling of abandonment, I feel the trap your mind put you through in an endless loop, I feel the torture you put yourself through quietly in your mind. It shouldn't have been easy, maybe you thought we were better off without you in our lives, so you persisted on your drinking until death. Let all these parts of you be healed and forgotten and with every small victory your kids achieve on this earth may you shine brighter in the sky. I always believed that we are one existing in two bodies, let me start where you ended and let me end, where you wished you could have ended it.

Felt like I was enlightened my body felt like a feather, felt like I was lifting off from the sofa I was sitting on as I have found my purpose, my reason to live. Happiness flooded my heart and I felt like I met my soul. I began to think back at the last decade of my life and the memories I had. Little did I know my journey would end like this, I was chasing success and money and thought I would end achieving them but instead all I got was a change within myself which felt infinitely better. I felt like I already had it all even without having anything to show for. All the moments from the very start till now couldn't have made more meaning to me until this moment. I valued every moment and knew deep down inside of me no matter which path I took I would have faced these challenges only in a different way. It was because of the path that I took and had the experiences that I had, that shaped this man I was now. Most times in the past when I had such a change in my life, I would be excited that a good change is coming into my life, but I would also be scared because I would think it would be tough and I used to be full of self-doubt. This time it is different, I am so calm and excited I have no clue what is to come or how I will achieve my dreams, all I know is, no matter what may come it's going to be beautiful and I'm going to enjoy it no matter what.

Felt like just a moment passed since the period I was struggling with addictions that turned by life into utter chaos, there were moments when I thought I will never survive this nightmare as I couldn't live a day without using those silent killers, I am in total clarity now completely free from its clutches. Felt like everything changed in just a blink of an eye, while it felt like an eternity of torture, pain, and disappointments while I was dwelling in my destructive patterns. Time is such a strange thing, how we experience time felt like it depended on my emotion. During the dark struggling days, it would feel like the torture was endless as time moved so slow despite noticing days fly by. And now I feel like time has stopped weirdly, and time is yet so short that I can't do enough for a day. There was a time when I will pray for the day to end but it takes its time to end and nowadays, I pray it doesn't, and it ends so quickly. I was at the cusp becoming the new me, it did take more time to grow out of my old ways. Though I never relapsed, mental battles were fought to bring me to the path that mattered and were won effortlessly. I was finally able to give the fight back to old patterns that have brought me to this point of change, now it was time to win without falling to old ways out of old habit.

Gradually as the days went by and the momentum build in the right direction the feeling that I succeeded filled me. I no longer had to think too hard or fight against myself to keep me in track I was flowing free and doing things effortlessly which caused a great deal of happiness. The small things mattered and doing the small things brought peace and happiness. During my cycles of self-destruction doing these small things were dreadful and boring, and I was constantly scared and worried that I will screw things up eventually and things turned out that way. Everything that seemed impossible to achieve became possible when I broke them down to small doable actions, I was able to accomplish them easily, the small things. Before I used to take drastic measures to re-compensate for the damage I would have done against my progress and end up messing things up further. Now I just let things be as it is and keep moving in the right path I should be taking.

There will be a period you will need to give yourself for things to pick up momentum and propel you in the right direction. Most of us are too eager to make it happen immediately and just when you were beginning to make progress you give up. Don't expect miracles if you aren't willing to give the time for it to happen. For instance, don't keep checking your weight when you're trying to lose weight, instead keep doing what you must do and built the habit of consistently maintaining healthy lifestyle which will help you in the long run. Otherwise, you will get frustrated by the process of losing weight or after you have done so you will fall back to your old fat assed self, if you don't maintain it as a lifestyle choice. The amount of time for you to reach your goals is entirely upon you, it's literally in your hands, the more dedicated you are the easier the process. For losing the weight you desire doing the necessary work in order to achieve it must be as addictive as eating a cup cake or pizza. And then maintaining the result will happen only when you embrace the working out and healthy choices, and you enjoy them way more than stuffing your mouth with cupcakes or pizzas. Until you learn to enjoy the things you dread, and you know in your heart is the right thing to do nothing will change. And until you take that faith of leap you will keep falling back to old ways and don't worry if that happens. If you learn to not quit one day you will succeed. I would spend time concentrating on changing on aspect I wanted to change and once I succeeded, I'll add another and then another. It doesn't take that much time compared to the time you spend in your destructive ways or even the times when you are second guessing; once you're all in and you're relentless then anything is possible and the possibility of it happening sooner becomes stronger.

Once you're in the flow of life everything happens with such ease, you are never in a desiring state there, you exist as someone whose desires have been already met. You think and act in complete trust with the universe and the universe never ceases to disappoint you. In order to get to this state, I had to learn to trust all over again and it was a challenge. I did revolt and question the universe, but the more I let go and just did my part and let the higher power do its part everything aligned to manifest in its own divine timing which made it all the sweeter. And even before I knew, few months later, I woke up a completely different man. It didn't take another decade just a couple of months. I was a nuclear power plant of pure blissful life.

I don't have all the answers of the universe; I don't know what the journey must be for you to take. All I know is once you truly begin to believe in your self-something miraculous happens and all you need to do after this is follow your heart; this experience is difficult to explain as it must be experienced to understand it, to understand what it truly means to believe in yourself. As a soul I began to feel as though I were a spec of energy connected to everything, I was just a tiny part of this colossal thinking being inside whom we all are in. This was an experience I felt while I was high on LSD couple of years back. I was in at The Kite's place; I don't remember how the trip began all I remember was waking up right in the middle of it. It was as though I was asleep until suddenly, I was awakened by a very deep voice that seemed to come from everywhere and this being revealed itself to me. In my head, its proportion or size is unfathomable seemed like it extended forever until infinity. It was a loving, smoothing voice that spoke to me with so much love, it understood all my pain and it consoled me. This giant being identified itself to me as "Brahman," who is the creator, the creator of everything. It revealed myself within itself and all I could see was a tiny light among countless among lights within itself. He spoke to me with love and care, I was floating around in space, I could see universes coming into form and some falling part, I could see intelligent life forms in various planets, scattered around the cosmos. Everything was light just like me in a finite shape within Brahman. Brahman enquired about my life on earth and asked how I was doing there, he showed immense pleasure to having met me and wanted me to explore the space as much as I wanted. I roamed around the cosmos and this deep voice guiding me telling me about the cosmos. I was a tourist, and he was my guide and I glided past stars and planets, the views were breathing taking, with the light breaking down to different colors and mingling together to form more complex colors all sprayed around like clouds beautifully flowing into one another. I saw life forms in other planets some less evolved than us human's and other more evolved.

And then there was divine beings of lights, angels, that assisted Brahman create universes, planets, stars, and life forms. They were all humming in a deep soothing sound that seemed to be the vibration of the light I was made of. I did not feel separate from anything but a small part of the whole. I felt what Brahman felt, I thought what he thought, I listened to his thoughts and plans he had for the universe, planets, and life forms. Finally, I approached a giant lotus in space and in this lotus was water which reflected the cosmos and right in the center of the lotus was a blinding light. As I approached this source of light it got dim, and a humanoid form revealed itself that was made of light like my body. Welcome it said, you have finally made it, the first thing I asked was if I was dead or dreaming and the humanoid form which was Brahma laughed, he laughed so heartily I too began laughing and then the diving light angels began laughing. All my pain and fears back on planet earth were gone I felt completely cleansed and free.

"No, my son, you are home with me," he said. We spoke in every detail of my life, and he would burst into a loud laugh whenever the comical parts of my life were discussed and then he would cry when I told him of my sorrows and painful experiences. He came forward and hugged me and told me it was an immense pleasure to have met me after such a long time, he was fond of me and had so much faith in me and told me not to worry at all, "For all good is to come," he said. And he gently laid his hand on my shoulder patted me and suddenly I woke up on the floor, drenched in my sweat. The whole experience felt like it took a lifetime, but I was out only for a couple of hours. But from then on this was how I always related and understood what this energy inside me was. It was a very powerful experience but once again it was just an acid trip which left a lasting impression of what god is in my head. I tried several other times to go back there and meet Brahman, but it never happened and eventually I gave up using LSD when my friend moved to another country.

I don't know why I decided to write this book, it happened spontaneously one day, and I just kept writing. This is just a simple story of a boy who wanted to understand his father's addiction and ended somehow finding his soul. I have no name, no color, no religion, I'm just a soul who have recognized itself and is taking its first baby steps since it's conception. I do not know where life will lead me next but I'm excited to embark in this new journey. I'm an energy and I am learning more about it as days go by. If this book must mean anything, let it be a drug that leads you to the only addiction you develop which is life, and allow your addiction to be a pure fun filled joyous expression which you contagiously spread around the world and where you creatively contribute. Let this soul's story inspire you to awaken you to the mystical depths of your own soul. May you find the way to your own soul who is waiting for you to acknowledge it and do not misunderstand this book as an opportunity to explore drugs. You don't need to, and I would advise against it, I experience the mystical part clearly and much more enjoyable while I'm sober now, and best part is I remember every bit of it, and I love my life.

Every moment in your life is an opportunity for you to turn your life around in a way you thought it was never possible. In order, for it to move in that path you need to believe in the impossible, you must allow the impossible to happen to you and guess the only way to get there is to ask the universe to show you the way to your real self and trust me the self will know what to do. We live on a planet where there are souls that have achieved impossible things in their lifetime, even to this day there are people doing impossible things and this ability is possessed by everyone, you are no different. Even if it's not great feats of creation, living from a place where you seem infinite and abundant by itself would be a liberating experience. And as one soul changes the another, imagine the impact we can make on this planet. To all you dreamers, misfits and the ones struggling to find your place on this planet it's time to take that leap of faith that you secretly crave, and you know deep down inside you, you can feel it in your bones that there is so much more to you but for some reason, you hesitate.

I drove to the old steel bridge on the far end of the beach connecting the mainland to a small island. I remembered standing there several times in the past when teenagers jumped off it into the waters below. It was a good 30ft jump down and every time I stood on the ledge, I would climb back up to safety even when I wanted to jump, I couldn't for some reason. Today as I stood on that ledge looking down to the waters below; nothing else crossed my mind but to jump. A few of the regular kids who often visited the place recognized me and started laughing, asking, "Are you going to jump? I dare you to jump."

Mocking me. I looked back at them and smiled, looked down at the blue stream of water flowing and I...